THE
BILLIONAIRE'S
THE INTERN TRILOGY BOOK 2
MISTAKE

paige press

THE BILLIONAIRE'S

THE INTERN TRILOGY BOOK 2

MISTAKE

lia hunt

Paige Press
Leander, TX 78641

Ebook:
ISBN: 978-1-953520-66-1

Print:
ISBN: 978-1-953520-76-0

PROLOGUE

EMERY

I SHOULD'VE KNOWN I was totally and completely doomed. I mean, I've always had terrible luck, but this was just peak screwing up at the worst—and I do mean *worst*—possible moment. I shouldn't be surprised at this point. Take a look through my history and you'll find at least 37 examples of me being the consummate screwup.

Mom would say I'm too hard on myself. Everybody messes up now and again, and sure, they do. She's not wrong. But after doing the bravest thing that I've ever done in my life by moving to New York, I've already jeopardized my job. I'm not talking about jeopardizing by like, stumbling through a presentation or anything, either. No, no. I didn't even get more than five feet from the elevator before I managed to truly and totally screw everything up.

And how did I do it? What was my weapon of choice for clobbering my career?

Coffee. A damn tray of coffees.

I'm lucky I didn't burn the guy. *That* would've been a lawsuit on top of a lost job. And it's such a good job, too. A dream job at Duke Capital. Well, a dream internship, but still. After all, I might not know exactly what I want to do yet, but

I know that this is the place to find out. And it's not just that Duke Capital is right in the middle of the city I've been fantasizing about for years. There's an energy here. It crackles with every step, every moment. Back in Kansas, everyone and everything moves slowly. There's no rush. Just kick back and watch life flicker by. But not here. Here, if you want something, you've got to seize it.

I'm ready to seize. I'm ready to live, and take chances and grow and experience life.

If only I could get out of my own damn way.

I glance across my boss's desk. Blythe Lawrence-Duke. She's one of those impossibly stunning women who seems like she was born wearing a carefully tailored power suit, perfectly manicured nails flashing as her hand flies across her open planner. I've been in this office for maybe ten minutes now, just waiting for her to finish writing whatever essay she's penning into her planner, but it's not so bad. At least it gives me a chance to collect myself and my thoughts. Though, really, I'm not doing much collecting. More like worrying that I've nuked my chances at success before they even got off the ground. All because I let my clumsiness get the better of me.

Of course, my two left feet weren't entirely to blame. No, blame must be placed on the unfairly attractive man that had to materialize in front of me at exactly the wrong time. God, he was so crazy hot. I know people think small town guys have all the charm, all the strapping farm-boy muscles, but I completely disagree. When he stepped in front of me, before I even knew who he was, I could feel his power. It radiated off of him, pure and total sex appeal from the broad set of his shoulders to the sharpness of his jaw to his eyes. Gah, his eyes. Piercing and molten, like he could seduce me with a single glance. And, honestly, he sort of did. At least, I felt heat pool between my legs, felt everything tighten just with one sweep of his eyes over me.

God, I wanted him. Pathetic, right? Lusting over some guy

the moment that I saw him. Candace, my cousin who's basically the sister I never had, would've made fun of me for it. She would've said it was my inexperience. That if I would just give it up and get some, I wouldn't be so eager because a hot guy glanced my way.

Except it wasn't just any hot guy I bumped into. Of course not. It's never that simple.

It was Harrison Duke. Namesake and CEO of the company I'm interning for.

And my boss's *husband*.

So, of course, I spilled coffee on him. I spilled coffee on him and—as if that wasn't bad enough—I felt *something* for him. Lust. Excitement. Attraction. Call it what you want. The point is I'm going straight to hell. Do not pass go, thanks for saving me a seat, Satan.

She must be pissed at me for being such an embarrassment. She can't be pissed about his suit because she's definitely not the kind of woman to drop off the dry cleaning. Ugh, wait. That was terribly sexist, to assume she should be responsible for the dry cleaning, just because she's a woman.

Of course she shouldn't.

Also, word around the office cubicles is that they're separated. Which I'm sure is very difficult and none of my business.

So this is not about the dry cleaning.

I wonder why they're separated though?

But really, none of that explains why I'm sitting in my new boss's office, squirming. And thinking about things I have no business thinking. Was this some kind of power display? And, if it was, what the hell was I supposed to do?

I glanced around her office, trying desperately to figure out something to say.

"And I'm done," she says, saving me from whatever pathetic attempt at conversation I was about to make. She sets down the pen and steeples her hands together, looking over those perfectly manicured nails at me. My own plain, naked nails are, thankfully, hidden in my lap.

"Ms. Mills," she continues, flipping her gorgeous, perfectly highlighted blonde hair over her shoulder. "Thank you for being patient. I have so many balls in the air. So many fires to put out. So many details to chase. You know how it is."

I smile. I appreciate hard work. Hard work was how I was raised, and from the moment I could walk, I was doing what I could to help my family. I admire that in Mrs. Lawrence-Duke. She could easily afford to be a lady who lunches. Yet here she is, working every day, running the charity department at Duke Capital. It's admirable. Inspiring. She smiles back at me, and I notice now that she's looked up from her planner that her eyes... Are they a little red? A little puffy? Oh God. Has she been crying? Is she about to deliver bad news?

They must be downsizing, I think. She's hired me only to find out that they don't have the funds. It's a last-in, first-out situation. I've read about those in the business books I checked out from the library. Basically, I'm screwed.

Maybe, if I play it cool and confident, she'll still give me a solid recommendation. That's all I can really hope for right now, anyway.

"I understand," I say, trying to keep the misery and anxiousness out of my voice. "I feel the same way. Hard work is important. Dotting the I's and crossing the T's."

She nods. For a moment, she just studies me, looking me up and down. I wonder if she can tell that I bought my outfit for today at the TJ Maxx near my new apartment. I know it's not New York couture, but I think it looks passably okay.

"Tell me, Ms. Emery Mills," she says, leaning back in her office chair. "What do you know about my husband?"

I blink. That wasn't what I expected her to ask. Except, well, maybe I should've. This must be about the coffee incident. She's pissed. She *is* planning to fire me, but not because she has to. Because I'm a total airhead who dumped coffee on her husband who happens to be the owner of the company.

I gulp. "What do I know?"

"Yes," she says. "A smart girl like you. I'm sure you did your research before starting here. So tell me, what do you know about Harrison Duke?"

I bite my lip and then straighten up. "Well, he inherited a small investment company from his grandfather. And then he built it into the international conglomerate it is today. He doesn't appear to be very interested in celebrity because he doesn't grant many interviews." Or more like zero interviews. At least in the last several years. I found a few old ones back when he was still building the business.

Mrs. Lawrence-Duke nods. "And what else do you know about him? Anything…personal?"

Ugh. She's talking about the coffee. She has to be. That, or she's reading my mind and she wants to tell me to stay away from her husband. As if she'd have to. I'd never. Never. Ever. I'm ashamed enough for the inexplicable wave of attraction I felt after slamming into him. Which is hardly my fault. That was just pure chemistry, chemistry I'd never, ever actually act on. I just have to fess up about the coffee and explain that I took the necessary steps to fix it. That's all I can do.

"Well, I know that I, um, spilled coffee on him this morning," I stammer. "Which was a total accident, and obviously, if I'd seen who it was, it never would've happened. Not that I think I should be spilling coffee on anyone. No one. But, um, I mean, the point is…well, I'm very sorry. I will of course pay for dry cleaning and—" That's it. The dry cleaning. They probably did have a fight about who should take it. "Do you want me to drop his suit off at the dry cleaners?"

Mrs. Lawrence-Duke holds up a hand, and I can't tell, but I think she might be holding back a smile.

"Calm down, Emery," she says. "I'm not upset about the

coffee mishap. It's fine. And I'm sure Mr. Duke has...well, don't worry about the dry cleaning or anything else. What else do you know?"

I take in a breath and think. Do I know anything else besides the fact that he's the most panty-melting guy I've ever met? I wrack my brain.

"There's the foundation, obviously," I say. "The one he founded in memory of his mother who always took him to work at the soup kitchen on holidays."

"That's the public story," she says, nodding again. "Please call me Blythe, by the way. Mrs. Lawrence-Duke seems so formal. And *old*."

Her eyes seem to shine under her perfect liner before she continues.

"What most people don't know is that when they say he *built* the company, he did it by being completely ruthless. He acquired failing family companies and stripped them for parts, selling other people's inheritances at a profit. He doesn't want people to know much about him because he's made a lot of enemies. A *lot*. And this foundation is *my* dream. He doesn't care about other people. He wants to control everyone around him, especially me. His only interests are money and sex."

I blush at that. I never walked in here expecting to hear about my boss's sex life, let alone her sex life with the CEO of the company. I don't know what to say, but luckily or unluckily for me, Mrs. Lawrence-Duke—Blythe—continues.

"He's just as ruthless at home," she says, dabbing at her eye with a tissue plucked from a silver-plated box on her desk. "I don't know if he ever loved me. I'm a possession to him. Sexually...he's rough. He cheats on me, controls me... But I haven't been able to catch him. All I want is my freedom."

The last word grabs me. Freedom. It's exactly why I first started dreaming of New York all those years ago. I'd look at pictures of the Empire State Building and—as cheesy as it seems—the Statue of Liberty and think, that's it. That's where I can really spread my wings and find myself. That's where my life can begin.

And then there's the rest of what Blythe just said, the parts about Harrison Duke being an asshole and a cheater. I should be surprised, but then, my own dad's both of those things… so I know. I know the lengths men will go to, pretending to be one thing while being another. The thought makes me shift uncomfortably since, just minutes ago, I was focused on how scrumptious Harrison Duke seemed.

I deflate.

I'm a terrible judge of character.

I'm not sure why I'm surprised. Even the best-looking men can be the biggest snakes. The most successful men often are. Every girl in the world knows that. Even the farm girls from Kansas.

"I want to divorce him, of course," Blythe says, drawing my attention back to her. Her eyes are definitely shiny now, and I don't know what I'll do if she actually starts crying. Thankfully, she stands up, still dabbing with the tissue as she looks out her window down on the city.

"I want to," she repeats. "I'm trying to. But he won't sign the papers. He's dragging it out, forcing me to stay married to him. He's stonewalling me and trying to leave me without a cent. I'm stuck. Unless…well, unless someone can motivate him…I don't stand a chance."

She turns and looks at me, a sad smile on her face. I feel so bad for her. I know what being stuck feels like. I know what it was like for my mom. Sure, I've never been stuck in the gilded cage Blythe is stuck in, but still. I can't imagine the stress she's under.

"I want to get to live my own life," she says. "That's all. That's not so much to ask, is it? All I need is the right person to help me."

I blink at her. Her implication's clear that the person she's talking about is me. But how could I help her? I'm just an intern from the Midwest. I don't know a thing about high-profile divorces.

"I would pay you," she says, as if that's the cause for my confusion. "Generously. It's the terrible irony, I have all this money as long as I stay. How's fifty thousand?"

Fifty...fifty thousand? Does she mean *dollars*?

"I'm sorry," I practically sputter. "But what are you talking about?"

She laughs. "Oh dear. I thought I was being rather obvious."

She comes back to the desk, and I see a flash of red bottom heels before she sits down. Then, she leans forward, her eyes flashing again—though this time, it's not with tears. It's with promise.

"I need you to date my husband."

CHAPTER ONE

EMERY

WHY, why didn't I just tell him what was going on?

Just add it to the growing list of things I've messed up because of Harrison Duke. First, the coffee. Then, every moment I'm with him. Every time he walks into the room I forget how to be normal. I forget how to do anything except soak him in. It's like all I can do is attempt to steady my own heartbeat as my body reacts to being near him. He's just...just the thought of him, of how he held me last night... I could fall apart right now. It's like I can still feel the pressure of his fingertips, how he trailed his hand down my back, how he gripped my ass in his palm.

How he slid inside of me and, just like every time we've been together, I felt myself shatter before he put me back together, again and again. It was like...well, sex wasn't anything like I'd thought it would be. I suppose there's that, for starters.

Not that anyone can know what it's going to be like until they actually experience it, but still. I never expected it to feel like *that*.

Far worse, I never expected to actually fall for him. Of course, from the first moment I saw him, covered in coffee I'd spilled on him, I'd thought he was hotter than hell. But there are plenty of men I've thought of as hot over my life. Like movie stars or famous athletes or even that one particularly attractive teacher I had my sophomore year in college. But I'd never expected to, you know, have coffee with any of them. Let alone spill coffee on them or have an actual relationship. And Harrison Duke? A literal billionaire? Yeah, it wasn't going to happen.

Until it did.

I remember the first time he kissed me, the first time I felt like, *holy crap,* he likes me. How he seemed to know just what I needed in a kiss, and how he was more than eager to give it to me. I'd kissed guys before, of course I had, I wasn't that naive. But it was never anything like kissing Harrison. Ever. *Ever.* Harrison was in a league all his own. He taught me that I'd basically been operating at half power my whole life, and with him, I was fully charged and eager for more. Eager to learn. As long as he was touching me, I didn't care. I needed more of him to breathe.

Dramatic bullshit, I know.

But you haven't kissed Harrison Duke.

I tried to stop it. I tried to just focus on all the terrible things Blythe said about him. That's why I'd agreed in the first place. Girl power and all that. I tried to focus on my deal with Blythe. Seduce her husband. Intrigue him just enough to incentivize him to finally sign the freaking divorce papers, so she could be free of him.

That was the deal, basically. I was never hired to sleep with him, of course not. Blythe made that explicitly clear. Just flirt and tease and remind him that being single would be a whole lot more fun than dragging their divorce on forever.

The joke really would have been on Blythe if she'd actually hired a freaking virgin to seduce her husband. Not that I'd ever have admitted that to her. How embarrassing. No, instead all I'd done was sputter the word *me???*

"I saw the way he looked at you," she'd said, with an indifferent shrug. As if telling me she thought a man like *her husband* would look twice at me. Or even once.

It was oddly flattering, in the way very fucked-up things are flattering. Is that a thing? I suppose not. But somehow it had seemed like a good idea. Fifty thousand dollars to flirt. I'd been…flattered. Flattered that anyone would think that I'd be capable of capturing the interest of Harrison Duke.

And he was supposed to be a jerk.

So it'd be easy, right?

It should've been so cut and dry.

Except, he was nothing like I expected him to be. Nothing like Blythe described. And no matter how much I tried, I couldn't dislike him. Not when I got to know him. Not when he showed me who he really was. Which was a real person. A real person who cared about me. Who looked at me like I was someone important to him, and not just some intern he was fooling around with. Harrison looked at me like I was everything.

Which is why, right now, I need to come clean. I have to tell him the truth. All of it. No matter how much I'd like to avoid it, and no matter how ashamed I am to have gotten myself into this situation. I have to make it right. I *will* make it right.

I look in the mirror, taking in my appearance. I've changed for dinner into a little cocktail dress, the kind that I know won't last long on me. The kind he might, if I'm good—or maybe if I'm just the right amount of bad—rip off.

God, that man. That impossibly sexy man.

Will he understand? Will he hear me out, when I confess? When I apologize for doing the most terrible awful thing to the last person who deserved it? I hope so. He has to know that I would never have done it if I'd known him, really known him. If Blythe hadn't filled my head with so many lies. If I hadn't been so naive to believe her side before having his.

Because now, of course, I know the truth. I know that Harrison wasn't the cheater. He wasn't the one who fucked around. It was her, and she doesn't even try to hide it. How many times have I seen her in her office smiling while talking on the phone to that guy, Robert? And now, now I know that he and Harrison were friends. Best friends. Because it wasn't enough, apparently, for Blythe to decimate her own relationship with Harrison. She had to destroy his best friendship, too.

Can you imagine? Losing your wife and your best friend in one fell swoop?

It's terrible. My heart aches for his loss. Yet in a way, in a terrible way, I have to be grateful that Blythe destroyed her marriage with Harrison. If she hadn't, I'd never have been with him. Like, ever. Would I have found him attractive? Of course. But if he hadn't been available—and by available I mean if his soon-to-be-ex-wife wasn't paying me—I'd never have dared to flirt with him.

I'm not that kind of brave.

I can't even imagine having pursued him on my own. Nope. Honestly when I think of all the awkward flirting I've done with him, I'm mortified. How on earth did it even work? I have zero flirting skills. And yet, he likes me. He likes me, a normal girl from Kansas…who only had the courage to pursue him for a paycheck. Ugh, gross. I sound like the worst person in the entire world. And a bit like a hooker.

You had good reasons, I remind myself, even as a blush of shame covers my face. I stare at my own reflection and fan my face with my hand, trying to calm myself. *Very good reasons. These student loans weren't going to pay themselves, and then there's Mom.*

I bite my lip just thinking about her, back at home, stuck in that house with all those chores. With the farm to tend to and so many bills piling up. I came here to New York to do something about all of that, dammit. And instead…

Instead I fell in love.

No, that's not all I've done. I know Harrison's not lying when he says that I'm good at my job. And I've studied my ass off to be here. And with a little time, I know I can make something of myself. I might not build a company like Duke Capital, but I know I can do *something*. Something to make Mom proud. To make everyone proud, including Harrison.

I just have to tell him everything. Right now. I never even cashed the check. That should count for something, right? Blythe gave it to me, what, a week ago? And I haven't even touched it. It's still there, just waiting to be shredded, still on my dresser—

Shit.

Shit!

The check.

My dresser.

My bedroom.

My bedroom where Harrison's waiting for me to finish getting ready.

I'm sprinting out of the bathroom, barreling down the hall before I can stop myself. I hear my roommates laughing in the other room, completely oblivious to me and my troubles. I bang open my bedroom door, breathing hard. It doesn't matter what I say to Harrison. I just have to get it out.

Only, he isn't here. It's not a big room, and it doesn't take more than half a second to see that he's gone.

And that's when the panic sets in. I turn to the dresser and walk to it the way I imagine they do in horror movies when they know they're about to discover the killer. My steps are slow and terrified, and when I get close enough, I feel like all of the breath is about to be sucked out of me.

But it's fine. The pile of mail is there, exactly as it was when I left. The check's near the middle, buried under some bills and ads and whatever. He didn't see it, then. He couldn't have. Not the check or her awful note. Unless he did…and he put it back?

No. No. I'm overthinking. He didn't see it.

Except.

He left.

Calm down, Emery, I tell myself. *Breathe. Breathe. Normal breaths. In and out.* Maybe he went out to get some air. Maybe…maybe an emergency came up. I check my phone to see if he texted me, but there's nothing. Heavy worry settles in the pit of my stomach, and I dare to peek into the living room-kitchen area. I half hope that I'll see him hanging out with my roommates, but he's not. Obviously. Why on earth would he be?

One of my roommates, Sherri, peeks up at me through glazed eyes. Apparently, they added pot to the mix since I last saw them. "You looking for your suit?"

I nod. "Did you, um, see him?"

Sherri giggles at the others. "Oh, we saw him. He looked really pissed, didn't he?"

The others laugh, and the worry in my stomach does several flips.

"Did he say anything?" I ask.

But it's no use. They've collapsed into a fit of giggles, and I know I won't get any answers from them.

I take to the halls, and then to the stairs, and I force myself not to call out his name. I'm letting my own anxiety about telling him the truth make up these horrible scenarios in my head, and none of them are grounded in reality. But when I get to the street and find that the car's gone, the terror really starts to set in.

I'm about to start crying right there on the sidewalk when my phone buzzes. It's Harrison, a text lighting up my screen like a beacon of hope.

Harrison: **Something came up. Have a good night.**

It's sparse, and it doesn't do much to settle my nerves. But at least...this must mean that he didn't find the check, right? He's just busy. Because he's Harrison Duke, and sometimes, things come up.

That's all it is, I tell myself. *Just New York business.*

But somehow, I know that's not true.

CHAPTER TWO

EMERY

"I NEED to return this check to you."

I got up before six this morning so I could get to Blythe's office before anyone else did. Well, actually, I barely slept last night. I kept replaying everything with Harrison from yesterday over and over again, knowing there was something important that I was missing. But whatever it was, there was only one course of action in my mind: give Blythe back the $50,000 and tell Harrison the truth. Whatever happened after that, I'd have to live with it.

Across from me, Blythe sits with her feet crossed one over the other on her desk, her sharp, patent leather heels glinting in the light. She's leaning back in her chair and eyeing me closely. We've gotten comfortable over the past few weeks. Or, more exactly, we were comfortable. Then, we were tense because I realized she'd lied to me about Harrison. Then, we were awkward. Or I was awkward because I didn't know what the hell to do.

Does she know? Does she know I've fallen in love with him? Or that he's fallen...in something...with me? There's something about the way she's staring at me and about the way her red lips are curving up that tells me she does know. Or, at the very least, she thinks I'm in over my head.

Which, whatever. She can think what she wants. I just want to close this chapter and get back to Harrison. I want to put this terrible decision behind me, and it starts with severing this deal.

I have to be careful, though, because she's still my boss. I might have Harrison in my corner, but this is where it gets messy. I have to break off this deal while also not pissing her off. It's a delicate balance, but I'm going to do my best.

"I'm sorry," I say, and then I wince. What am I apologizing for? I don't need to apologize to her.

She just watches me, eyes narrowing slightly as she continues to smile. She's waiting for me to explain, to trip over my words like the wide-eyed, innocent Kansas girl I am.

Oh, to have just an ounce of her confidence. To walk confidently through life like I own the world. But then I think about it, and no, I don't want to be anything like Blythe. I don't want to screw anyone over just to get a little further ahead. I don't want to break anyone's heart with such careless indifference.

"It's just… I don't feel good about it anymore," I say. "It's gotten too…"

Blythe nods as if she understands. "Too personal?"

I swallow. If I answer that question honestly, I'll give myself away completely. Besides, "personal" doesn't begin to cover my relationship with Harrison.

"I just don't feel good about it," I repeat. "As much as I appreciate your confidence in me and the opportunity… I just… I need you to take the money back, please."

I slide the check across the desk to her, but Blythe's eyes barely flick down to it before they return to me.

"Emery," she says, her voice a casual purr. "Why would I take the money back when you've done such an incredible job?"

I hate that my eyes prickle at those words. Because I know —and she knows—the implication of what she's saying. I've done an "incredible job" because Harrison's genuinely, and publicly, interested in me. Someone's spotted him, I'm sure of it. After what happened in Sun Valley, that much was clear. That lawyer would've told Blythe. In other words, Blythe likely thinks he's ready to grant her the divorce and she'll get whatever it is she wanted.

She doesn't know what I know, though. She doesn't know that Harrison's already told me that he's moved forward with the divorce on his own. Or maybe Blythe does know, and that's why she thinks I've done an incredible job. I don't care. I just want out of this office. I want out of any part I played in this. I want to get away from the sickening smell of her perfume. It's suffocating in here.

I force myself to look her dead in the eye. I steel myself and take a breath. I will not cry in front of this woman. She can't know that she's gotten to me.

"It was wrong for me to do in the first place," I say, still trying to sound as polite as I can. "I was in a low place. I was desperate. And—" I cut myself off before I admit the worst of it. That I was stupid and flattered.

Blythe arches an eyebrow. "And you're no longer desperate?"

I bite my lip. She knows that that's impossible. In the beginning, when she was pretending to be my friend, when she was acting like she really cared about me, she got me to talk about myself. About my family. About my mom and all of those bills.

"You deserve to be happy," she'd told me. "And Harrison…well, he's got money to burn. But he's selfish. This is how we win, Emery. This is how we beat him at his own game."

The words make me tense up just thinking about them.

She'd been so convincing that this was the right move, but I know now just how wrong she was. Just how wrong I was for falling into it. How greedy and stupid I was.

"It doesn't matter," I say. "I've just…changed my mind. So, please, take the check back."

She rolls her eyes, the first crack in her friendly façade.

"Oh, Emery," she says. "Do whatever you want with the check. Rip it up for all I care. Did you really think you needed to tell me that you weren't going to cash it?"

My cheeks burn. "I wanted you to know that I wasn't taking it. In case…"

She laughs, high and tinkly. "In case Harrison asks me? Oh, you naive girl. How little you know about Harrison. Or, no, that's not right. You do know a fair amount about my soon-to-be-ex-husband. But remember, Emery. What you know about him, you know because *I* told you."

Her words send a shiver up my spine. An embarrassed, ashamed shiver. Because in the beginning, when I was "seducing" Harrison, I was using her advice. I wore the clothes she told me would draw his eyes. I made the moves she told me he'd respond to. At least, I tried. Honestly, I was pretty clumsy with everything. And I know it wasn't just because of Blythe's advice that we fell for each other. Harrison and I, we have something special. Something pure.

You know, outside of all my lies.

But I won't let Blythe make me question it. Not for a second.

"If you won't take the check back," I say, trying to sound stronger than I feel, "then I'll destroy it myself."

I take it and rip it cleanly down the middle, and then I drop it into her trash can. She watches me with an amused expression. It makes me want to claw her eyes out. How did I ever trust her?

I stand up and turn before I can say anything else to get

me into trouble, but before I can reach the door, Blythe clears her throat. I turn back to her, and she smiles a sad sort of smile.

"Emery, I want you to remember that I've been where you are," she says. "And I know he probably seems great right now, but he's not. That honeymoon phase you're in with him will crash and burn. And when it does, I want you to remember that I warned you. I never meant for you to get hurt. Truly."

Her lies hang in the air between us, waiting for an answer. But I'm done listening to her. I'm done letting her tales poison the reality I have with Harrison.

I exit and yank the door shut behind me, letting the walls rattle a little behind me as I leave. It's true Harrison form, and I like to think he might even be proud.

And speaking of Harrison, he must be in the office by now. I know he might not get here as early as Blythe—something I know because that's when we used to plot, if I'm being honest—but he must be getting in soon. Especially with the Pink deal so freshly inked and so many details still to be sorted.

I force myself not to skip to his office, even though I want to run straight to him. Because getting the truth out between us is going to be freeing, and once it's out, he'll know that I really, truly love him. He'll see it radiating off of me because, after talking to Blythe, I know one thing for sure. What Harrison and I have is real. The moments between us, those were all real, even if my clumsy seduction was a bit manufactured. I'm not perfect, and I hope he'll forgive me for that. I hope he sees the truth in who we are together, despite this messy, imperfect start. That's what love is, after all. It must be.

I'm right that he's in the office. I see the light on, and I even catch sight of him through the door that's slightly ajar. My face splits into a total grin, and I don't even care how goofy in love I must look to Sandy, his assistant. I catch her watching me with a smile, knowing that she's been rooting for us the whole time.

See, I think. *We're meant to be.*

I'm almost to the door when I hear another voice. A female voice. I watch Harrison cross to his desk and rifle through some paperwork, and then I see the woman across from him. It's the lawyer from before. Claire. She's angled her body with her hands on his desk, the sight of her ample chest front and center if he were to look up. Jealousy sparks inside of me, but I swallow it down and knock on the open door.

"Um, Harrison?"

He doesn't even glance up. He keeps going through the papers until he finds one, and then he zips a pen across the bottom to sign in. Claire looks at me and then at Harrison, but she doesn't say anything. I guess she said everything she had to say when she told Harrison he needed to stay the hell away from me in Sun Valley.

"Harrison," I say again, and finally, after this, he looks up.

"Did you need something, Ms. Mills?"

His voice is cold, so icy and unlike the usual warmth he uses when we talk to each other. It's rude, even. I've never heard him speak this way, to anyone, except maybe in that first meeting with Pink when he was putting some sexist asshole in his place. I've definitely never heard it sound like this when he's talked to me.

Which makes all of my worries from last night resurface. Did he see it? Did he see the check? And if he did...

"Ms. Mills," he says, sounding annoyed now. "I'm extremely busy. Is there something I can help you with?"

"Well," I stall, looking at Claire. This isn't the kind of thing I want to talk about with her here.

"I'll just go," Claire says, clearly picking up the hint. At least she didn't try to lecture us. That's the last thing I need right now, especially with how weird he's being.

"That won't be necessary," Harrison says, looking up to

give Claire his full and undivided attention. Something about that look tightens something in my chest. Something very, very bad. "Whatever Ms. Mills needs to say, she can say here in front of you."

His eyes flash, and then a small smirk plays out across his face.

"Though, I suppose if you're in a hurry, Claire," he says to her, while looking at me, "we can continue our conversation tonight at dinner."

Immediately, every part of my body goes cold. He's having dinner with Claire? I must be hallucinating...or misinterpreting, at the very least.

Claire raises an eyebrow. "Okay. Will do. I'll see you then, Harrison."

She glances again at me, and then, with a click of her heels, she's out of the door. Once she's gone, I whirl back on Harrison.

"What the hell was that?" I ask. "Harrison—"

"Harrison what?" he cuts me off, with a raised brow as if somehow I'm the one being ridiculous.

"You're having dinner with Claire?" I question, and then just to make sure I'm crystal clear I add three excruciatingly painful words. "Like a date?"

"Oh, you thought we were exclusive?" he says, sounding bored. He even adds a look of confusion, which seems genuine. "That's not how we do it here, Kansas."

If everything inside of me froze before, now, it shatters. Because those words, they don't make sense coming out of his mouth. They're impossible.

Unbidden, Blythe's words come back to me.

I want you to remember that I warned you.

But no. It couldn't be. He couldn't be.

Except, when I look in his eyes, there's no love there. There's nothing but coldness, nothing but boredom. I can't bear to look at it for any longer before I turn on my heels, biting back the tears, as I flee his office.

CHAPTER THREE

HARRISON

THE SECOND EMERY LEAVES, my feet move automatically to follow her. It takes the memory of finding that check on her dresser to stop me from running after her, and I have to remind myself that, even now, this is part of her performance. She doesn't give a shit about me, and she never has. It's all been an act to get paid. To get paid by Blythe, my total and complete shrew of an ex-wife.

Ever since I found that check, I've imagined what happened with her and Emery. I've been such a besotted idiot I'd have come up with ten excuses for the money, but the note really sealed the deal. Imagining the details of their arrangement is worse than not knowing because, now, every memory is tainted by the knowledge that it was guided in some way by Blythe. Did Blythe tell her what to say at that dinner? Did she pick out the outfit? Or did she leave that to Emery? When did she even interject? Has it all been a lie, or just part of it?

I push my door shut before Sandy can come in and ask what's going on. Hell, I don't have an answer for her. Thankfully, we closed the deal with Pink already, and I can afford to put some of my other work off. Not for long. But at least for the time it takes to wrap my head around this bullshit.

It's the lies. It's the same spiral I went through with Blythe, wondering which of her late nights or her excuses were real and which ones were just cover-ups for fucking my best friend. Only now, this feels worse. Which doesn't make any damn sense because, really, I barely know Emery. It's my own fault for getting wrapped up in her, for letting myself get tempted by a young, hot piece of ass.

And to think, I actually thought I was in love with her. A woman I barely know. A sexy tempting little liar. I let myself believe in *love* again, even though I know better than anyone that it's all a lie.

I go to my desk and sit down, but then I'm up and pacing again a moment later. My whole body's running on adrenaline that has nowhere to go. I'd normally throw it all into work, but my focus is shot. Work does nothing but remind me of Emery and Blythe, since I still have the charity fiasco to wrap up. Not that I'm going to let that get fucked up. I don't care if that was part of the performance—Emery was right, no matter how much I hate to admit it. There must've been some truth in there, I guess. Some heart. Not that it mattered. Not that it'll do anything to revise my opinion of her now.

At least Blythe will be out of my life soon enough. It shouldn't have taken an intern for me to see that staying married to Blythe is more of a punishment for me than her. Still, even with everything that's happened, I still don't plan on giving her a thing I don't legally have to. If anything, her stunt with Emery's convinced me I don't owe her an iota of financial compassion. She's evil to the core.

It's exactly what I was just trying to tell Claire. I don't care what lawyer magic she has to do as long as Blythe leaves this marriage with everything she deserves—namely, as little as possible. Of course, I didn't get a chance to finish telling her that because Emery had to appear in the door, still trying to look helpless and innocent. As if I'm still buying that.

I shake thoughts of Emery away and pick up my phone to

dial Claire and finish our conversation. She picks up immediately.

"Harrison," she says, sounding more annoyed than I think is reasonable, being that I employ her. "Sounds like your conversation with Ms. Mills was quick."

"I'm not calling about that," I snap. "As I told you when you barged into my office this morning, that won't be a concern anymore."

"Joy," Claire says flatly. "Even though I don't believe you. And what was that about dinner tonight? We're not actually having dinner, are we?"

"Of course not," I say. "But I appreciate you playing along."

She sighs on the other end of the line. "Then what else do you need to discuss, Harrison? I told you that I'll need some time to get it locked up. Especially since you're insisting on the impossible."

"It's not impossible," I say, growling a little. "Not for someone competent. Are you saying you're not competent, Claire?"

"No," she says. "But, as I've told you, Blythe is entitled—"

"To nothing," I say.

Claire makes a sort of strangled noise. I pull the phone away from my ear and quickly scroll to my photos where a picture of Blythe's check to Emery shows Blythe's treachery clear as day. Not that I've shared this with Claire. Not yet. Still, it's a good reminder, one that I might, unfortunately, need to remind me that Emery was never who I thought she was.

"I have another request," I say, putting the phone back to my ear. "I want to talk to Blythe."

"Harrison, I told you, now that the proceedings have started, you have to keep your distance. For *your* sake."

"Yes, but this is important," I say.

"I can't condone it," she says. "And I strongly advise against it. Just let me do my job, okay?"

I nod, even though she can't see me. "Don't disappoint me, Claire."

There's some unintelligible grumbling on her end, and then the line cuts out. I consider her advice. I do respect Claire. I know what she's saying is sound.

But I also decide, fuck it, I need to talk to my wife. Now. She needs to know that I know about her scheme. I can't stand the idea of her thinking she has the upper hand for a second longer.

I stalk over to her office, avoiding Sandy's eyes and the eyes of the few workers who have taken their seats at their desks this early. I'm at Blythe's open door soon enough, and I don't wait for an invitation to be let inside.

She's at her desk, and from the moment she looks up, I know that she's been expecting me. It pisses me off more than it should. How do you make someone forget everything they know about you? How do you rip away the secrets you shared so that they can't use them against you?

"Harrison," she says in a breathy voice. "How nice to see you."

"How did you even find her?" I say, cutting off whatever poisonous pleasantries she was going to attempt to spin.

She doesn't even attempt to deny it or play dumb. Instead, she leans back and knits her hands together like a fucking cartoon villain. I half expect her to let out an evil laugh, but she just smirks at me instead.

"She was perfect, wasn't she?" Blythe says. "Sheer luck on my part. I saw the way you looked at her when she dumped coffee all over you and a lightbulb went off. I had no idea the whole 'innocent farm girl' bullshit would be such catnip for you but that spark between you was too good to ignore. You've always been so easy to fool, Harrison. So stuck in your own head you can't even see it. Still...I didn't realize you would fall so hard for the bait. You made it almost too easy."

"Shut up," I snarl. The shame inside of me is coiling around like a snake, and I don't need to start a shouting match with Blythe for the whole office to hear.

"And she was *so* coachable," she says, and then she leans forward like she's had a lightning bolt moment. "I should put that in her file. 'Very coachable. Excellent team player. Listens and takes feedback.' What else, Harrison? Maybe something about her being 'hands on'?"

If I were a different man, I would strangle her. She lets out a girlish laugh that doesn't suit her as I steam. It's the kind of laugh that would be so natural out of Emery, someone who truly *is* innocent. Or, at least, parts of her are. Or were. The virginity thing, for example. No way in hell that was fake. And what she shared about her brother...

Fuck, I'm getting in my head again. Whatever Emery is or isn't, there was collusion, and that's all I need to know.

"This was a cute stunt," I say, pointing a finger at her. "But hear this. It was just that. A stunt. And it won't get you anywhere."

"Oh, I beg to differ," she says, eyes twinkling. "Especially since you've been so...indiscreet."

The threat's there, a neon sign blaring in her voice. But I don't give a shit.

"You won't get a dime," I say. "And you sure as hell won't hold on to this charity. Your days here are numbered, Blythe. This is your one and only warning."

I don't give her the chance for a snarky comeback. I turn around and barrel out of her office, heading straight for the elevators on my way out.

If there was ever a day to work from home, it's today.

CHAPTER FOUR

EMERY

WHEN I WAS a kid and I had a bad day, Mom would always, no matter what was going on, drop everything and we'd get ice cream. I'd walk into the kitchen with my light pink backpack and my drooping pigtails, and she'd take one look at my face and announce that it was time for a trip to Joe's Scoop Shoppe.

We'd bundle into her old, battered Ford truck and rumble down the road, and we'd stay there until the chocolate chips and sweet cream beat away the bad of the day. Sometimes, if things were really desperate—like when I got bullied for wearing handmade dresses or when I didn't get into my first choice for college—we'd up the amount of toppings to include hot fudge syrup and freshly cut strawberries. But always, the ice cream fixed it.

So, when I make it to the end of the most miserable day I've ever had at Duke Capital with no sign of Harrison reversing course on whoever the heck he turned into this morning, I know exactly what my after-work plans are.

The ice cream shop I stumble into is no Joe's Scoop Shoppe. Joe's is a small place with a hand-painted menu and a mural on the wall that his granddaughter did. The ice cream's freshly churned, and if you asked Joe, he'd be able to tell you exactly which cow the milk for the cream came from. This shop in New York is different. Much like everything in New York is different. This place is full of trendy décor, right down to the neon "Scoops Up" sign. And the flavor selection is decidedly curated. Lavender & honey. Rosemary & olive oil. I manage to find a basic vanilla bean—albeit organic with imported Italian vanilla, but vanilla is vanilla, surely. I order a scoop, but when I taste it, it's icy and *too* cold.

I could walk home with my disappointing cup, but that sounds even more depressing, so I head to a nearby park for some clear air and space to think. Unfortunately, New York's not exactly big on the "space to think" thing. I find an empty park bench, but every five seconds there's a jogger or a fast walker or someone yapping on their phone as they do laps around the greenery. Normally, it's the kind of thing I love about New York. But today, it's making me feel like I might break out in hives.

What am I going to do now? There's no way I'll last another day at Duke Capital. If Blythe doesn't fire me, Harrison will. My chances of sticking around are as gone as my hopes and dreams. And why would I stay there, anyway? All day today, I'm certain I caught people staring at me. Whispered conversations that would cease when I got too close. Ramon was polite, but I think he knew the same thing everyone else did. That I'm a silly intern who fancied herself in love with her boss. I bet they're laughing about me. They probably had an office pool about how fast he'd get bored of the new, dumb intern.

God. And I thought I was special.

Part of me wants to be furious with him—*is* furious at him —for not even listening to me. I think about what Blythe said, and as much as I don't want to believe it, I wonder if she was right. If Harrison is exactly who she said he was: an egomaniac, a womanizer, an asshole.

But if he was, then how was it so good between us? How did he hold me and make me feel like my life was finally perfect? No one's that good of an actor. No one is that cold and calculating, surely? Except…me. When I was doing it to him.

Right? I got what I deserved.

I'm the one who entered that relationship with the wrong motives.

I became someone I never was back home.

Home. The place where people are simple and kind and not two-faced. Where I have an actual window that I can open all the way and look out onto our farm. Where the smell of fresh grass and hay and sunlight filter in, and where I wake up to a rooster's crowing and the sound of Jackson, my old horse, neighing from the barn.

Tears threaten to fall for the seventieth time today, but now, I finally give into them. I let the salty water tumble down my cheeks and into my bullshit "artisanal" ice cream, and then I pull out my phone and call up Mom as fast as I can. I don't bother with FaceTime since I don't need her to see me crying on a park bench in New York.

It doesn't matter, though, because as soon as I hear her voice, there's no hiding the sound of my sobs.

"Baby," she says. "What's wrong, honey?"

What can I say? Mom, I tried to save you and our home by taking a job from a woman to seduce her husband, but it didn't work out because I fell in love with him but the joke was on me because he really is a giant asshole? Mom's always been understanding, but there are some things that I just never, ever want her to know.

"I'm a wreck, Mom," I say instead, hiccupping and shaking. For once, I'm grateful that nothing phases New Yorkers. No one even gives a passing glance to the girl having an emotional breakdown in the park.

"What's going on," she asks. "You're the bravest person I

know, moving across the country by yourself. But if anyone can handle it, it's you, Emery. I know you can."

I cry harder, shaking my head even though she can't see me.

"No, Mom, I can't. I'm a total failure."

"Did you lose your job?" Mom asks, her voice immediately panicked. She knows that, without my job, we're both screwed.

And it's all my fault.

"I...I just..."

I stare at my ice cream, melting in its sad cup in my sad lap. It tastes cheap and artificial, and I want to chuck it across the park. But then I feel guilty because this ice cream cost six dollars, and as I'm already barely making enough to get by here, I better eat the damn thing.

It's that detail, that ridiculous realization, that completely breaks me. I might've been pretending to have it all together when I was with Harrison, but I don't live on Park Place. I live with roommates in an apartment that's the size of one of Harrison's closets. And as much as I've tried to make it mine and make it cozy, and as many times as I told Harrison that I loved it, the truth is, I'm sick of living in a shoebox. I'm sick of trying to fit in somewhere that, let's face it, I just don't belong.

"I want to come home," I tell Mom. "I *need* to come home."

I hear her breathing on the other line. I wait for her to tell me that, nope, no way, I just need to push forward and try a little harder. But it doesn't come, and maybe that's the worst part of all.

"Okay, sugar," she says. "You can always come home. Get yourself on the next plane. We'll make this right. Together."

"Can we get ice cream?" I ask pitifully, looking at my melting scoop. "At Joe's?"

"Of course we can," she reassures me. "First stop after the airport."

CHAPTER FIVE

HARRISON

"TELL me again why you want to be in this meeting?"

Ramon's been suspicious of me ever since I returned from Sun Valley. Or, more exactly, the day after I returned. This is the problem with getting close to anyone. They know you. Ramon doesn't even know me that well, and he's still able to pick up that something's wrong. He doesn't ask about it directly. Instead, he raises an eyebrow and questions every damn move I make.

It's infuriating, but I can't call him on it without revealing that I know that he knows that something's off. And he at least has the decency to not call me out in front of anyone. Like now. He's waited for my office to clear of Sandy and the executive that I called in here, the one I'm going to terrify by sitting in on her meeting unannounced. It's one of our tech investments, something I usually don't get involved with at this level, and she must think I'm about to fire her.

I shrug. "I haven't sat in on one of these in a while. You know I like to be involved."

"Sure," Ramon replies, the word carefully measured. "But you and I both know that this project is running smoothly and it's a waste of your time. Are you worried about something?"

I shake my head. "Of course not. I just want to see how it's going."

Ramon's eyes narrow just a little. Not in an angry sort of way, but in a way that tells me he's running the numbers on why I might possibly be jumping in right now. He must be evaluating the client, the outside influences...everything.

And then, unfortunately, he lands on it.

"I asked Emery to join this meeting," he says. "Jesus, Harrison—"

"It's not what you think," I say. "I only want to evaluate her."

"Evaluate what?" he asks and I don't miss the sarcasm. "She's only sitting in to observe and take notes."

"Then it really doesn't matter if I'm there," I snap, and before he can say anything else, I cut him off. "I'd like to attend, Ramon. And that's all there is to it."

I *am* the CEO, and my voice and my words both remind him of that fact, so he sighs.

"You're right, boss," he says. "I'll see you there in a bit."

I adjust my tie once he's gone. Is it petty that I'm dropping in on Emery's meeting? It's petty as hell, but I don't care. Watching her squirm yesterday, making her feel some of the pain that I felt the other night...it's all that's getting me through right now. If I stop to think about what happened after the squirming, the tears that I have to tell myself were as fake as her whole performance, then the guilt threatens to settle in. But I won't let it. I need to remind myself that Emery was nothing, a blip, a mistake. And I need the entire office to know it, too. That there's nothing to see. No drama, no...nothing.

When it's time for the meeting, I walk in and take my place at the head of the table. I walk with power, reinvigorated from the deal with Pink. I try not to remember that it was Emery's help in that last minute that secured the deal. Instead, I focus on the fact that it's my name on the building. My work that's built this company. My work that will safeguard and protect it for years to come.

The others watch me, waiting for some sort of bomb to detonate, but it doesn't come. I stare straight ahead and wave for them to begin, and then I let Ramon do the rest of the work. The entire time, I watch the door, waiting for Emery to appear with her little notebook.

Only, she doesn't appear. She never shows. And when the meeting is over, Ramon shoots me a look. An accusatory look.

I refuse to engage with him, instead, I return to my office. Because I have to force myself not to go looking for her.

For the rest of the day, no matter how hard I try not to, I can't shake the memory of her tears from my brain.

———

THE NEXT DAY, I decide I have to see her. Just a glance, just to see her reaction. To feel out if she's avoiding me or still calculating her next move. I could ask Ramon where the hell she is, but that would be feeding into his fixation, so I decide to do some digging of my own. I walk, casually as I can, over to the break room. Just the sight of it reminds me of her, of her soft curves pressed against me, of her hand running down the length of my abs, finding their way to my hard cock. Other memories spring up in recognition, memories of her crying out my name as I pressed deeper and deeper into her. I force the thoughts down and continue my casual walk past where I believe her cubicle is located, but when I'm there, I can't find it. And the longer I stand around, the more curious looks I get, so I abandon the plan.

I could ask Sandy. She and Emery seemed close. But that would look pathetic. I won't be acting like a lovesick puppy searching for a scrap of affection. That's not what happened, anyway. I'm just a man looking for answers, that's all. Not even the answers. Just...why the hell wasn't she here yesterday?

Then it hits me. HR. Yes, I can ask HR. It's perfectly reasonable for the CEO to ask questions about an employee. Fine, maybe it's not at all reasonable but fuck it, it's my company.

I wander over to that department acting as nonchalant as possible. I step up to a random desk, and the assistant sitting there looks up from her computer and nearly falls out of her chair.

"Mr. Duke!" she squeals. "I, um—"

Her supervisor's skirting over to save her before she can sputter her way into foolishness.

"Mr. Duke," the supervisor, a curly-haired woman named Whitney, questions. I'm surprised I know her name. Because with all my "it's my company" bullshit, I don't actually pay any attention to HR details. I especially put them out of my mind when I decided to fuck an intern.

One look at her raised eyebrow tells me she's surprised to see me. Surprised and concerned.

"Should we go into my office?" Whitney asks, gesturing behind her.

"Not necessary. I wanted to check in about an employee," I say, absently picking up a pen off the assistant's desk. "One of the interns, a young lady by the name of Emery Mills. She was supposed to be in a meeting yesterday."

It's such bullshit. Whitney and the assistant exchange a look.

"Of course," she says. "Ms. Mills. Well, um, Mr. Duke... she quit. Yesterday morning."

Quit? It seems impossible, and my first thought is that Blythe might've interfered. But these aren't thoughts for me to process here in front of HR. So I nod, not bothering to thank them, and head back to my own office. Behind me, I can practically hear Whitney rolling her eyes as she sighs, so I walk faster.

Once in my office, I shut the door. I stare at the city, then turn away and stare at the wall. Looking at the view now reminds me of Emery and her ridiculous doe-eyed fascination with it. Her belief that this was the place where things happened and where anything could be achieved. It was bullshit, and I knew it. But she didn't. She was still innocent.

Innocent, but not so innocent that she wouldn't go into cahoots with Blythe. Something about it doesn't sit right with me, especially now with this news that she's quit.

She's running away. Running, because she knows, deep down, that what she did was wrong. That she crossed the wrong man.

But still, I expected her to try a bit harder. Come up with some halfhearted explanation. Tell me she did it because of some bullshit or other. Blame Blythe, maybe. But instead, she's just left without even attempting to salvage our relationship.

The thought stops me in my tracks. I hadn't even realized I'd been pacing until I grind to a halt. Did we have a relationship to salvage? Everything happened so fast, it's all whiplash at this point. I bought a ring for fuck's sake. Clearly I was out of my mind to have done so, right? All of the memories of us whirl together, all of the nights we spent together, every meal we shared, every smile she graced me with. Even our decision to make it official, to go for it, it's all so recent. Was any of it real?

Yes. As devastating as the answer is, yes.

She slept with me. There's no way in hell that was part of her deal with Blythe. It's not even logical. Why would Blythe have hired an innocent to seduce me? It's not like I've got a particular, if any, fetish with virgins. The thought actually makes me smile for a moment. Blythe never hired amateurs for anything. What a fuckup of a hire that was.

I don't have the full story here.

Emery and I had something. She can't deny it. And neither can I.

So how in the hell was she able to just leave without an explanation?

CHAPTER SIX

EMERY

I EXPECT to feel lighter the moment that the plane touches down in Kansas, but as the wheels slam into the runway, all I feel is heaviness. It's like New York followed me here, sticking to me like gum to my shoe.

I ended up leaving a bunch of my stuff with my roommates. It just wasn't worth it to pay to have it shipped. Most of what I arrived with fit back in my suitcases. But the bedding and towels I so carefully picked out at the Home-Goods on the Upper West Side and lugged home on the subway were left in New York. The beautiful clothes that Harrison gave me? I definitely left those too. My roommates happily claimed them, promising to show those outfits the good times they deserved. It felt cruel to abandon it all, but truthfully, I don't think I can stand any more reminders of Harrison Duke. Not when he's still burned in my brain, every memory we had together playing on repeat.

I work my way through the airport, dragging my beat-up carry-on bag behind me. I've got a checked bag with the rest of my worldly possessions. My entire sad life fit into a couple of bags. Though honestly what's in there isn't worth much. I'd probably be better off if the airline lost my bag and had to pay me, because I need every last cent I can scrape together at this point.

I can't give up on helping Mom. It might not be the same dream as New York, not as flashy or as instantly successful, but I can find something here in Kansas. Hell, I'll scoop ice cream at Joe's if he'll hire me.

I might want to avoid coffee shops, though. I've already proven that I can't be trusted with hot beverages. God, even coffee reminds me of him. Will everything always make me think of that asshole?

If only it were easy to think of him that way. Because every time I try, I get a random memory surfacing of him smiling or laughing or paying my student loans or donating to the charity that saved my brother. I want to think of him as all bad. It would be easier that way.

But unfortunately, Harrison does have some decency. And I saw it, too much of it, and now that's all my brain wants to focus on.

I grab my bag from the luggage carousel and head outside to find Mom already at the curb, waving at me from her truck. I run over and toss my bags in the truck bed, and then I haul myself up into the front seat. Immediately, she's yanked me into a hug, squeezing me hard as I breathe in her cherry-scented perfume. There's also the smell of grass, probably because she was mowing, and a little bit of hay, too. I wonder if she went riding.

Ugh, riding. I can't wait to get on a horse and just take off into the sunset. Just me and Jackson and none of this real world bullshit.

"My baby girl," Mom says. "I missed you."

I won't cry. I've already cried way too much these last couple of days, and I've decided I'm not giving Harrison Duke another tear. He doesn't deserve them. Not now when I'm home, safe, and ready to start my new future.

Mom drives slow on the way home. I don't think she

means to. In fact, I think this is how she's always driven. But after New York, everything feels like it's moving through molasses. Even the way people walk feels slow. Slow, slow, slow. And the closer we get to my town of Cottonwood Falls, the slower everything feels. Cottonwood Falls. Home. If the sign's to be believed, we're still hovering at a population of 910. That means there's a pretty good chance that every single person there knows me, or at the very least, they know my mom or my brother.

Or my dad. I guess they might know him, too, though no one ever talks about him.

"I've got a surprise for you," Mom says. "Waiting at the house. My God, you look skinny, Emery Jane."

I roll my eyes. I've always looked skinny to Mom.

"I hope it's a hot bath," I say. "I feel like I've still got city grime all over me."

"It's better," Mom says with a wink. "Trust me."

With my luck, it'll be a man. Mom's always seen a man as my way out, which is ridiculous because that's definitely not how it worked out for her. Still, she loves me, so when I said I was going to New York, she didn't put up too big of a fight. The thought strikes me that maybe she knew I was going to fail and that's why she let me go, but I push it away.

Once we get to the house—after a scoop at Joe's, of course —I see that the surprise is better than both a hot bath *and* a man combined. Because running down the stairs is the only person I have ever been able to be myself around, the person who used to watch silly movies with me while we ate never-ending bowls of popcorn. The person who knows all my secrets, including my New York ones.

Or most of them anyway.

"Candace!" I scream, exploding out of the truck so that I can run to her and wrap her in a hug. Her wild brown curls are pulled back in a messy bun, and she smells like dirt and hay. When I pull back from her, I see there's a fresh dusting of freckles across her nose and tan lines peeking out from under her tank top.

"I told you," Mom says, winking at me. She grabs my carry-on from the trunk. "Why don't you two girls go for a ride? I bet you have a lot to talk about."

I smile. This is why it's so great to be home. Mom knows me, and she's picked exactly the right solution for what ails me right now: my best friend and a ride.

It takes a few minutes to get Jackson and one of our other horses, a dapple grey mare named Pebbles, ready to ride. The whole time, Candace watches me knowingly, waiting for me to spill the New York beans. I kept her up to date right up until things got bad, and then I just sent her a message that I was coming home.

But as for why? I hadn't gotten there yet.

We take laps around the trails near the house, and I fill Candace in on everything. How Harrison broke things off with me. How I tried to give the money back to Blythe. How he's apparently been fucking the lawyer behind my back because we weren't exclusive. Through it all, Candace's face changes from shock to annoyance to complete rage.

"He was fucking the lawyer?" she snaps, pulling Pebbles to a halt. "This is the same guy you thought you were falling in love with, right?"

I groan. "Yes. And I hate to admit it, but I think his ex-wife was right."

"Fuck," Candace says. "And you already ripped up the check? You should ask for another one for all this suffering."

"No way." I shake my head. "I don't want it. I'm putting it all behind me. God, like I could ever think that New York City was for me. Can you imagine?"

Candace laughs. "Hell no. This is where you belong."

I nod, but I bite my lip. How can I tell Candace, who's always been a Kansas girl through and through, that New York also, impossibly, felt like home? That part of me did love the falafel carts and the yellow taxis and the giant buildings? That a part of me came alive in that city? She wouldn't get it. And besides, that part of me was wrong. Tempted by the grandeur of it all, but utterly and completely wrong.

"Well, let's race home," Candace says. "I need to make sure I can still whip your ass."

"Excuse me?" I grin. "I'm pretty sure I was the one who was always beating you."

She winks at me, and then we're off, racing through the woods, the dying Kansas sunshine falling across my skin like a blanket.

I'm home, I think. *I'm home, I'm home, I'm home.*

If only it felt right.

CHAPTER SEVEN

EMERY

MOM WAKES me up at the crack of dawn the next day, and for a second, I think she's going to make me do chores just like when I was a teen. Not that I'm not willing to pull my weight. In fact, cleaning out the trough and tending to the chickens might be just the thing to get my mind off certain Manhattan billionaires who, from here on out, I will refuse to name.

But she's not. Instead, she's hanging up the clothes from my carry-on, idly examining them as she does.

"Mom!" I say as she plucks a cocktail dress out, her eyes widening. "Why are you going through my stuff?"

"I'm not, hon," she shrugs innocently. "I just thought I'd help you get settled in again. But Emery, where did you get this?"

It's the cocktail dress that I was going to wear to dinner with Harrison that night. I thought I'd left it with my room-mates, seeing it was a gift from him. Not a Blythe hand-me-down. Something he'd actually had sent with me in mind. I could still imagine his hands running along the tight material, how he would run his fingertips along my thigh before—

I shake my head and refocus, reminding my depressed,

horny mind that I'm back in my childhood bedroom with my mom. Not exactly the place for dirty thoughts.

"It was a gift," I say, waving it away. I'm sure she's already spotted the designer label and recognizes it as nothing I'd have bought on my own. "It's whatever."

"A gift from…"

She raises her eyebrows. Somehow, Mom also got the memo that we're not speaking his name.

"It doesn't matter," I say. "But anyway, I'll put everything away after I shower. Do you need help with the chores first?"

"Oh no," she says. "You've got a brunch date, missy."

"With whom?" I ask skeptically, scrunching up my nose, not bothering to hide my frown.

Mom just smiles. "Take a shower. I'll put this all away. And I found one of the old sundresses you left behind. So cute. I'll just put it out with some sandals for you."

I resist the urge to scream. I tried to donate those sundresses, but somehow, they didn't ever make it to the Goodwill. And I'd put money on it that it's my mom's favorite dress of mine, a flouncy thing with cherries on it and straps that tie at the shoulders. And if I'm right, and that's the dress, then that can only mean one thing.

Mom's got a date planned for me. Candace was a—much appreciated—decoy, but the real surprise is going to be exactly what I was worried about. A man.

I sigh, but I do as I'm told and head into the shower. The shower here is a little roomier than the one I shared with my roommates back in New York. Everything is a little roomier here. And it's nice to have a bathroom to myself, too, and not have to fight over drawer space. These are the things I remind myself of when I start wistfully thinking of life back in that apartment, the one a certain someone referred to as shitty and small.

I gather my hair into a messy bun and eye the dress Mom's laid out for me. It is, indeed, the cherry-pattern sundress, and I glare at it and all of its implications. I might be back home, but I'm not just slipping back into my old life. I went to New York, dammit. I learned some important lessons. And, fuck, I just don't feel like wearing that sundress.

Instead, I dig out a pair of cozy jeans and an old, baby blue T-shirt. I slip into a pair of worn sneakers, feeling very comfortable and also very not-date-like. No matter who's waiting for me in the house, I know that my heart won't be in it. And this is just the outfit to tell them that.

———

I'M RIGHT. It is a guy. A very nice guy who I know very well, and the smile that splits my face when I see him is genuine. It's Pete, a guy I grew up with. He was a couple of years ahead of me in school and I thought he'd moved to California, but apparently, he's also found his way back home. I'd ask him about it, but I don't want to open that can of worms —especially not when it will inevitably work its way back to me and asking why I left New York.

Pete takes me to the local diner, and he orders enough food for several people, including blueberry pancakes, biscuits and jam, eggs, and bacon.

"I have to eat a lot," he tells me. "To keep my stamina up for my job."

He's a firefighter because of course he is. He's got the kind of body they'd put on a calendar, all thick biceps and stomach muscles that peek through his tight shirt. He's got a friendly smile and soft, bright green eyes. There's stubble on his chin and calluses on his fingertips. He's a Kansas daydream, and yet, sitting across from him, I feel nothing.

Apparently, loving a certain New Yorker has completely destroyed my sex drive. Something else to hate him for.

"I bet," I say, forcing myself to pay attention to Pete.

"Though, if I remember right, you always had a healthy appetite."

He laughs, low and deep. "You don't forget a thing, do you, Emery?"

He says my name like a low rumble of thunder.

"I remember a certain pie-eating contest," I say. "And how you promised me you were going to eat seventeen slices of pie."

He winces. "Oh God. And I remember you promised me a kiss if I actually ate them all."

I giggle. "Yes, I did. Though I'm pretty sure you only made it through five."

"Seven!" Pete says, laughing. "Such a failure. It's no wonder I never got that kiss."

His eyes twinkle, and I force myself to look away. I don't want to hurt Pete. He's got to know exactly what this is: my mom being a ridiculous matchmaker, and me coming back home with my tail tucked between my legs.

I bite my lip and decide to just rip the bandage off.

"I just got out of a, um, heavy relationship," I say.

Pete nods. "I'm sorry to hear that. He's a dick, obviously."

I laugh. How do I answer that? I guess I can be semi-honest.

"A bit," I say. "But part of it was my fault, too."

Pete's eyes watch me, steady and clear.

"Maybe it just wasn't a good match," he says.

I sigh. It's true, and it's the easiest, simplest answer for what happened. *Maybe it just wasn't a good match.* It leaves out the betrayal, the lies, the heartbreak that's left. It also leaves out the passion and the feel of my back against the shower wall, of wet skin sliding against mine, of a pressure building inside of me. Of the way I felt held and safe when it was all over.

Maybe sex is always like that, I wonder? Would sex with Pete be the same? Not that I'm considering it, but now that

I'm thinking about it… Did I believe that what Harrison and I had was special because I had nothing to compare it to? Somehow, I don't think so.

And fuck, there I go thinking his name again.

"Let's talk about something else," I say. "Mom told me you're helping your family out here."

He nods. "My dad's got bad arthritis, and I'm helping him with the day-to-day. It's funny, I never pictured coming back here. When I left, I thought I hated this place. It always felt so suffocating. But now that I'm back, I can't believe I ever left. It just feels…right."

Something cold passes over my heart. Pete's looking at me, waiting for me to agree. But the words don't come, even though they should.

I force a smile. "That's great."

He nods and reaches across the table, tucking his hand around mine.

"I'm really happy you're back, Emery," he says. "Cotton-wood will be more fun with you back in it, just like the old days."

I spend the rest of the meal forcing food into my mouth, trying to focus on the solid, handsome, reliable man before me. I keep my eyes trained ahead, seeing but not really seeing. Because all I can think of is another man, a man who's very presence seemed to ignite me into being.

If only he were here, my traitorous mind thinks, and then I shove the thought away before it can really take root.

CHAPTER EIGHT

HARRISON

WHY HADN'T she even tried to tell me her side of the story?

Once I started thinking about that, I really hadn't been able to stop. The thought of it on repeat in my mind.

At first, I tried to beat the thoughts out of my head with the punching bag in my private gym. Each punch ricocheted through my muscles, rippling through my biceps and back through my shoulders. I pounded it again and again, hoping that physical exhaustion would take over and leave me to sleep in peace.

But it didn't. Instead, I dreamed that I was in the gym. And after exhausting myself with that stupid bag, I turned, body thrumming with energy, and there she was. Emery. Standing there in skintight black leggings and a tiny scrap of fabric that had no business calling itself a sports bra. I've never seen her wear such a thing, but my dream self has both a vivid imagination and an adept memory of everything Emery. She approached me with a coy smile, sweat glistening on her skin as if she's just finished her own workout.

"Join me in the showers?" she'd purred.

She gave me a wink and swung her hips as she turned, and I followed her hungrily to the locker room at the back of the gym. It has dark black tiles and a rainfall showerhead, and she stripped her clothes off as she approached it. She dropped each piece of clothing on the ground until I was staring at the smooth, muscled curve of her ass and the shape of her hips. She stepped in and let the water fall across her body, and then she faced me, beautiful and perfect in every way.

I pulled off my own clothes, and then I went to her the way a starving dog went to a buffet. I caught her face in my hand and nipped at her jaw, turning her head up as she released a sigh. I ran my wet hand up her stomach and cupped her breast, finding her nipple hard and perfect. I flicked it and she groaned. With my other hand, I traced circles along her hipbone, and she arched forward, urging me inside her. Fuck, I wanted her. I knew that her wet pussy would welcome me, would fit me perfectly, tight and slick. I aligned myself, and then her eyes flashed open.

Now, waking up from the dream, I can see that I'm going to have to beat this out another way. I'm sweating and my cock's demanding attention, swollen and throbbing with need. I push down my sweatpants and fist my hand around my own hardness, the tip already slick with pre-cum. I pump the flesh, thinking of the Emery from my dream. She's somehow not quite as off-limits as the Emery I know from life. She still looks at me with lust and admiration, something I suspect the real Emery wouldn't do at the moment.

I pump up and down, thrusting my hips to match the pulse of my hand, but the orgasm sucks and I'm left feeling frustrated rather than sated. God, what I want is a hate fuck to close the damn book with that girl. One last time to feel her, touch her, and thrust inside of her until she screams my name one more time. I want an ending on my terms, not hers. I need to fuck her out of my life.

I get ready quickly, not bothering with the shadow of

stubble on my jaw. This isn't a woman I'm trying to impress. This is sex and nothing more, as it should've been all along.

———

I DON'T BOTHER to call for Leo as Emery's apartment is less than a mile on foot. I need the walk to clear my head, and further, I don't need Leo to witness this. This…whatever it is. A premeditated walk of shame because I'm already annoyed with myself.

Yet here I am. Outside her apartment. The walk up her stairs brings up memories that are complicated and painful, mostly because the most recent memory I have is of the night I discovered her betrayal. A betrayal that still stings, raw, when I raise my fist and knock on her door.

One of her roommates answers. Her eyes are sharp and narrowed.

"You," she snaps. "The suit. What are you doing here?"

"I need to speak to Emery," I say, not even bothering to address her dig. "Now," I add when she just stands there glaring at me.

"How about never," she snaps back, crossing her arms over her chest. "You're despicable, you know that? Don't you think you've done enough?"

I'm tempted to sigh, but it's beneath me. I'm sure the roommates have a much different version of events than I do.

"Emery," I repeat, leveling her with the sort of look I usually reserve for enemies in boardrooms.

She looks over her shoulder as she calls out in an obnoxious singsong tone of voice for backup.

"Hey you guys! There's someone here to see Emery."

I wait for Emery to appear, eyeing her door at the end of the hall. But instead, two girls who are not Emery make an appearance.

"Ugh, him," one of them mutters, not at all discreetly. "What's he doing here?"

"Apparently, he needed to remind us in person that he's a giant asshole," says the other.

This time, I do sigh. An annoyed huff of breath to keep myself from being a bigger dick than they already think I am.

"I'm loving this sisterhood against dickbags thing you've got going on," I finally snap. "But can you just tell Emery I'm here." And then, because I am a dickbag I add, "And you don't know what happened."

"Oh, don't we?" asks one of the girls, her long hair falling in front of her eyes. She blows it out of her face and attempts to stare me down, then shrugs. "Whatever. Based on your having a dick, my money's on this being your fault."

I breathe in hard through my nose, trying to refrain from debating my level of assholeness with these strangers. That's not why I'm here. I look past them to Emery's room, and I debate just pushing past them. Then, my eyes catch on the girl I don't know, and I recognize something about her. No, not her. The blazer she's wearing. It's rolled up, and she's paired it with overalls of all things, trying to look eccentric but just looking like a child who wandered into their parents' closet. But the blazer—I know it. Emery had taken it from Blythe's abandoned closet.

"Emery's gone," says the roommate who first opened the door when I knocked. "She's not here, so you can stop looking for her, okay? Paige moved into her room."

The words don't make sense. Emery left? Where would she even go? Did she get a nicer shit box of an apartment?

The roommate with the long hair sighs. "Dude, she went back to Kansas. If you want to see her, go there."

"Or maybe don't," says Paige, the replacement roommate. "She can do better," she adds, eyeing me like I'm no one she'd swipe right on.

I'm about to defend myself, but I stop before I engage

further. It's not worth it. I'm the bad guy. Case closed. "Well," I say instead, attempting to add an ounce of charm to my words, "how about you just give me her new address, and then I'll be on my way."

Instead, they shut the door right in my face.

That visit went better than I'd expected, all things considered.

Once I'm back on the sidewalk, I make a couple of calls, the final of them to Sandy, telling her to schedule the jet. When she asks where I'll be going, I tell her "Kansas" and then hang up before she can say anything else.

Less than an hour later I've packed a bag and I'm en route to Teterboro, Leo behind the wheel. Despite my best efforts, he catches my eye in the rearview mirror.

"Would you like to stop to pick up a gift for Miss Emery? Perhaps flowers?" He looks hopeful, the old romantic fool.

I grit my teeth. "That won't be necessary, but thank you, Leo."

He just nods. "Of course, sir."

I sigh and look out of the window as New York's finest hotels and restaurants whip past me.

I hope they have a Four Seasons in this goddamn flyover state.

CHAPTER NINE

EMERY

THERE ARE some things that you never forget how to do. They come back to you without a thought, memorized by your soul. Riding a horse or milking a cow, for starters. Kissing someone, I guess, though some kisses—and some kissers—are obviously better than others. And there's one thing my body has certainly never forgotten.

Farmers' market day.

Or more specifically, working the family booth on farmers' market day.

Mom woke me up at four in the morning, and even though any reasonable person would be screaming for more sleep, my body knew it was a farmers' market day. Exhausted but jittery. The kind of feeling most people would associate with birthdays or maybe Christmas morning, or making it to the airport on time, and it carried me through my shower and getting dressed. Mom hadn't bothered to try to force another sundress on me. First, because my "date" with Pete was so disastrous, and second because no one wears a sundress to the farmers' market. No, today I was in a pair of worn overalls with rips at the knees and a pair of cowboy boots that I dug out of the back of my closet. I braided my hair quickly, and then I took a look in the mirror.

A few weeks ago, that reflection would've looked a lot different. I would've been wearing a combination of work clothes that I'd put together thanks to Nordstrom Rack and TJ Maxx, and I'd be trying as hard as I could to look like I belonged. Looking at me now, you never would've guessed that for a moment I was a city girl. A New York City girl. A woman with a big future. Today, I looked like any other Kansas girl ready to go help her family sell some corn —literally.

I helped Mom pack the eggs, the greens, the fruit, and— her specialty—different loaves of bread. Pumpkin, chocolate chip, lemon blueberry… They were all always guaranteed hits. Nothing had changed since I'd been gone, which made sense because, well, I wasn't gone that long. But there was still something about it that made me a little sad. Because it was so easy to slip back in.

Too easy.

We got to our designated space at the market, the same space we've had for longer than I've been alive, and Mom went around saying hello to everyone like she always did. Her smile lit up every person she visited, and people were eager to ask about the farm. Like us, I knew these other families depended on this day for funds to keep the lights on. Maybe some of them had kids off in other states sending money home. Which is what my mom should've had if I hadn't gone and messed it up.

I shake my head and focus on cutting up a few apples to offer as samples. Samples are key to getting your booth noticed. They're your hook for a new customer. I also cut up one of the lemon blueberry breads into cubes, but I'm a little more precious with it since it's a guaranteed best seller.

"Just about ready?" Mom asks me, putting an arm around me.

I nod. "Is Candace here yet?"

Candace has been helping Mom while I've been away. I'm grateful she's coming today because I need someone to steady me. Someone to remind me that I'm in the right place.

"Should be here soon," she says, and then she gives me a smile as she taps my cowboy boot with her own. "You look good, Emery."

I smile. I know she's disappointed that I didn't exactly hit it off with Pete, but she's being a good sport. At least, she hasn't sprung any random men on me again.

The farmers' market opens, and the first wave of customers filter in. Some folks recognize me, and others are drawn to my samples. They've heard Mrs. Mills makes the best bread at the market, and they're eager to get the freshest stuff. I chat with some of my old neighbors and schoolmates, but when they ask if I'm back for good, I don't have an answer. I barely have a smile.

Deflect, deflect, deflect.

I'm refilling a tray of apple slices and reflecting on the life choices that have led to me cutting apple slices today instead of I don't know, visiting a museum or eating falafel from a food cart or taking a walk in Central Park, when something catches me so off guard my heart nearly stops.

Harrison. Duke.

Is here. Standing right in front of me.

In Cottonwood Falls, Kansas.

And is he...wearing a freaking suit to a farmers' market?

Does he even know how to Saturday? I guess to be fair it's possibly a sport coat and slacks? Maybe? Or maybe he's not here at all and I've simply conjured a vision of him, like a genie, or a person hallucinating an ocean in the midst of a desert. Or a crazy woman dreaming up a billionaire in the midst of a rural farm town.

He's really here.

Why?

And why does he have to look so delicious even while he looks so entirely out of place? He smells good too. Familiar, in a very different way than hay and grass are familiar to me. In a very, very expensive cologne way. It's a rich, sharp smell, something musky and clean at the same time. I hadn't realized I'd missed even his scent until this very moment. It makes me irrationally angry.

"Well," he says, breaking the spell he's most definitely just cast over me. "Look what I found."

He reaches for an apple slice, but I yank the tray away and narrow my eyes.

"These apples are spoken for."

I don't know what makes me say it. Honestly, the words just sort of jump out of my mouth before they process through my brain. With how hard my heart's beating, I don't know how I'm talking at all. And what was I supposed to open with? *Hey, how've you been?*

Yeah, no.

And thank God Mom is wandering around chatting with the other vendors because I don't know what she'd do if she saw some suit she's never met standing here, talking to me. She'd piece it together real quick.

"Spoken for?" Harrison asks, raising an eyebrow. "Apples aren't generally exclusive, Kansas."

Oh, so we're doing this? Fine, Harrison. Fine.

"Then they should say so up front," I snap in reply, glaring at him. Without thinking, I pop an apple slice in my mouth, just to show him what he can't have.

His eyes narrow, but he shakes his head and glances around us, taking in the magnificent view that is the farmers' market. When he speaks again he mutters, "You're a hundred and fifty miles from a goddamn airport," as if that's somehow my fault?

"Yes, well, sorry you couldn't catch a direct flight to a farm, Harrison. Next time try a crop duster; if you don't mind roughing it a little, they can land just about anywhere out here."

"Hmm," he murmurs.

I'm being petty, and I don't care. But he doesn't take the bait.

"It's very, uh, 'authentic,'" he says, and then he glances at the bread. He picks up a pumpkin loaf and turns it over, examining the sticker on it. Mom makes them herself, and I'm pretty sure she designed it about ten years ago with clipart. It's a smiling woman next to a cartoon cow, and it says: Mills Baking Company—sweetest bread in the world!

I could die right here. Not out of joy. But because Harrison and his expensive clothing and his polished shoes are making me feel smaller than I ever have.

"I'd like to buy this," he says. "How much?"

"Oh no," I reply, shaking my head. "This bread is exclusive," I snap. God I'm an idiot. That doesn't even make sense. "Exclusively available to Kansans only," I add, because that makes it not at all less stupid.

A hear a laugh behind me and I turn to see Candace, grinning as she puts a crate of milk down on one of the tables. She's in the tiniest top I've ever seen and a pair of Daisy Dukes that fit her a little too well. She smiles and claps me on the back, and then she turns her eyes on Harrison and lets out a whistle.

"Where'd you come from, handsome?" Candace asks. "You're lost, clearly. Looking like that in a place like this."

I glare at her. She must've figured out who he is. Candace isn't dumb. I wait for her to start screaming at him, but instead, she just grins at him.

"You want some of this bread?" Candace asks. "This is my aunt's bread. It's the best. We usually charge six dollars a loaf, but for you, four dollars, seeing as how you must be a tourist."

Harrison smiles. I hate that he's smiling at her. I hate that he's smiling at all, honestly.

"I'll take one of each," he says. "Please."

"Well, that'll be twenty-four dollars, sir," Candace says. "Let me just go grab the cash box."

I follow Candace to the back of the booth and whisper-hiss at her. "What are you doing?"

"Making a sale," Candace says, rolling her eyes. "I know you've been gone, but that's generally what we try to do."

"No," I say. "Not to him."

"That's exactly why we sell to him," she says. "If you can't have him, you can at least have his money."

"Absolutely not—"

But then I stop in my tracks. Because Harrison's no longer the only customer at the booth. Another person has joined him, someone roughly the same height but wearing about half as many clothes, thanks to a faded old T-shirt and cargo shorts that hang perfectly on his hips.

"Pete!" I call, nearly falling over a crate of greens as I rush to stop any conversation between them before it can even begin. "I didn't know you'd be here today."

I don't know who Harrison's icy glare is meant for because it sweeps over me and then Pete and back to me.

"Hey Emery," Pete says, and then he pulls some flowers from behind his back. "I thought I'd bring you a little welcome home present. A thank you for yesterday."

Oh God. Oh God. Flowers? He had to bring me flowers? *Now*? I risk a glance at Harrison, and he looks murderous. But really? As if he has any right to.

"I grabbed them from a booth down the way," he says. "Figured you'd need something to smile about after—"

"That's so sweet," I say, rushing to cut him off. "And I'll get them in water right away. But I need to get back to helping Candace."

He looks a little hurt but nods. "Sure. Just call me later."

"Of course," I say, and then I wave like a fool until he gets the hint and walks away.

Yes, I'm playing it cool. Very cool.

"Here you go," Candace says from behind me, appearing with a packed paper bag to hand to Harrison. "That'll be $24."

Harrison digs into his wallet and pulls out a hundred dollar bill. He hands it to Candace and I can already see her frowning at it, I'm sure worrying about how breaking it will wipe out all of our change.

"Keep it," he says before she can argue. "I don't need change."

Candace's eyes stay wide as she looks at me, but then she shrugs and heads back to the till. I glare at Harrison.

"You shouldn't have done that," I say. "I don't need your charity."

"Oh?" Harrison says. "I wasn't sure when that was supposed to be over."

The accusation's a knife, and I take in a breath to recenter myself after the blow.

"Why are you here, Harrison?"

His eyes steady me, so deep and rich and molten. I wish they were looking at me differently. I wish they were looking at me like they did the first time I knew he truly cared for me, but he'll never look at me like that again. Unless... Why did he come here? Is it to apologize? Was Blythe wrong? She must be. Surely he didn't get on a plane and fly to Kansas to further explain how not exclusive we were. Right? He must be here because—

"I have some of your things," he says, interrupting my thoughts and crushing any last hope that I had. "I'd like to return them."

Ugh. Of course Harrison Duke would jump on his private plane to return my fucking things. This isn't anything to him. It's settling an open account, clearing an inconvenience.

Perhaps just a fun way to spend a Saturday, watching me squirm.

"Fine," I finally grit the word out. "Just leave them here."

He shakes his head and checks his Rolex. "I need to get them from my hotel. Can I drop them off when you're off work?"

I roll my eyes. "Farm work is never done, *New York*."

That unearths a chuckle from him that almost sounds genuine. But before I know it, his gaze is hard again.

"I'll meet you at your house," he says. "Would that be acceptable?"

What do I do? Tell him to go fuck himself? I should. Of course I should, but somehow, I can't say it to his face. I don't want him to leave. Not really. If this is the last day we share together, then I'm going to drag it out. If he flew all this way just to amuse himself, then I can amuse myself too.

"Meet me at the barn," I say. "I'll text you the address."

Suddenly, a spark of creativity hits me. I give him an innocent smile as I tell him, "You can help me feed the horses."

CHAPTER TEN

HARRISON

HELP HER FEED THE HORSES? Did she not notice that I'm not dressed for chores? Or does she not care? Given her fondness for destroying my clothes with caffeinated beverages, I suppose I shouldn't be surprised. And it's not like I can't buy more.

But still.

I could change before heading over there, but nothing I hastily packed would be any better suited than what I'm already wearing. Did I think to pack jeans for Kansas? No, I sure as fuck did not. I didn't think at all, clearly.

I didn't think about anything, except seeing Emery.

Which according to my dick was worth it, because I've got a hard-on from the memory of what she was wearing back at that farmers' market...those overalls. Stupid, baggy overalls. But I could make out the slightest curve of her ass beneath the denim. And one of the straps kept sliding down her arm and exposing a tight tank top beneath. Clinging perfectly to her chest. And those boots.

Apparently, my farm-girl jack-off fantasies have been eerily correct, and it's not helping anything. I don't need to be distracted by my dick when I've come here for closure. I need her side of the story, and that's it. Then I'm on the next flight out of Farmville, which luckily for me is whenever I want it to be since it's my plane.

I don't know why I told her I had her things. I don't have anything except my own damn suitcase.

I rented a car when I got here because, well because honestly I didn't have much of a game plan beyond the flight.

It's a Subaru Outback because apparently there aren't a fleet of luxury cars at the Kansas City airport. At least there aren't when you don't plan in advance.

The Subaru is good for me though.

I wasn't always a rich asshole, the reminder is nice. Besides, being able to drive my own car is giving me a strange sense of liberation. It's been a while since I've gotten behind the wheel of a car myself, and it's giving me at least one thing I can control. I've been doing laps around town to get a better idea of what's here and to kill time before I meet Emery at her barn. But honestly, there's not much to the town. A bunch of buildings that look like they belong on Kansas postcards, a couple landmarks, a church, and houses flung far and wide.

And, of course, plenty of cows. A few horses. I assume a bunch of chickens, though I can't see them from the road.

I decide it's time to get this over with and head for the address that Emery gave me. She's outside town, the kind of outside of town where they give up on paving the roads and just toss down some gravel and call it a day, apparently. When I finally find her address, I find an old house painted light yellow and white, with a red barn near the back and plenty of land spread out. There's a rooster for a mailbox and signage that says "The Mills" hanging in red letters above it, so at least I know I've found the right farmhouse.

Jesus, I didn't think about the fact that this was her family house. I hope her mom's still back at the farmers' market because I haven't had an argument in front of someone's mom since I was a teenager and I'm not in the mood for a replay of that today.

I park near the house and wince a little as I step out of the car and immediately get a splash of mud on my shoes, though I remind myself that I can buy more. I can afford thousands more. What I actually can't afford is looking the slightest bit put off in front of Emery. I already can't stand that she saw me vulnerable at any point in our farse of a relationship.

The window for vulnerability is over. I'm in control here.

I stroll up to the barn, the large wooden doors already ajar, the scent of animal and hay strong in the air. Inside a horse neighs and I peek into the slight darkness and find two rows of horses, a stretch of dirt and hay between them.

Then, there's her.

Emery.

The light filtering in through the barn has dust dancing in the air, and she's in the middle of it all, tossing hay into each horse's pen. As she moves, I see the toned muscles of her arms and legs move, her ass somehow perfect in those stupid overalls. One strap has again slid off her shoulder, this time far enough to reveal that the tank top below has inched up to reveal a sliver of her stomach.

Fuck.

Fuck.

My traitorous cock remembers those curves and what it felt like to thrust deep inside of her as she clamped her legs around me and moaned my name.

But that's not why I'm here, I remind myself. I will my dick to stand the hell down, though not with much success.

"Emery," I say, loud enough to grab her attention, even though my voice is low and gruff.

She whips around, her mouth forming a little "o" that sends even more blood straight to my dick.

"Harrison," she says, blowing a wisp of hair out of her

face. "I wasn't sure you'd…" She pauses. Thinks about her words, shrugs then simply says, "I don't know."

I close the distance between us, forgetting why I'm here, forgetting about the conversation we're supposed to have.

No, not forgetting.

Pushing it aside, because there's something else to do first.

I crush my mouth to hers, and she answers with a gasp, arching her back against me as she meets my furious kiss with her own. Our tongues and teeth clash as we devour each other, hungry and wanting and desperate.

"Get this ridiculous thing off," I growl, already sliding the remaining strap of her farm-girl lingerie down her arm.

She tugs me over to an empty stall, throwing open the door as we continue to kiss and grab at each other. My hands slide across her body, snatching at buttons and fabric. As we crash into the empty pen, I press her back into the wall, grinding my hard cock against her as she gasps. I reach under her bra and squeeze her breast, finding her nipples hard and aching. For me. I'm the one who undoes her this way. Me.

Her hands eagerly free me of my pants, and then those painfully soft fingers run along the edge of my cock before fisting around it, pumping the hardness slowly as I groan.

God, how I missed the feel of her touching me. She's no longer hesitant like she was those first few times. No longer needing direction or guidance or reassurance. In this moment, I can almost forget that I took her virginity and marked her the way that no other man will.

Almost.

There's an energy, an urgency about the way she's gripping my cock, like she needs this as much as I do. And hell, I hate to even think that I need it, but I know it's true. Need is coursing through me, driving me like a man starving and lost, and she's the only path home. And then when I think that, I remember her betrayal and how she pretended to want me because she was paid to.

Hate fuck, I remind myself. *I flew to Kansas for a hate fuck.*

The overalls have pooled at her feet, and she kicks them aside. pushed down during our initial frenzy of touches. She's in just the tank top and a tiny scrap of white underwear and I realize that I need to know if she's wet for me, if she wants me the way I want her.

I trace the elastic with a finger, and she shudders, her hand stilling on my cock as if she can't handle any other movement except the one of my fingers teasing the waist-band, sliding lower and cupping her. I can feel the heat radiating from her even through the fabric.

I need more of her. Need to know.

I slide them down her hips and slip a finger inside her, finding her gloriously, deliciously wet and slick. For me. For fucking me, no one else.

"Harrison," she gasps my name, and I relish the way it sounds coming out of her, knowing that I was right and she wants this as much as I do.

She arches forward, riding my finger as she continues to work her hand over my cock. But it's not enough.

"I want to fuck you," I tell her, and she gasps as I add a second finger. "I want to fuck you so hard you won't walk straight for a week."

She whimpers at that, her grip on my cock tightening.

"Yes," she says. "Oh God, yes."

I retrieve the condom that I stashed in my wallet on a very purposeful whim this morning, and Emery watches hungrily as I rip the black and gold package and slide it on. Then, I press her harder into the side of the horse stall and slide an arm under her leg, lifting her up so that her hips are at exactly the right angle that I need. I ease into her and she sighs, welcoming every inch of me as she tightens around my cock. I groan, hating that I love how this feels, hating how every inch of me sparks as her fingernails scratch at my back. I cup her ass with my hands as I drive deeper and deeper into her, and her first orgasm comes fast and hard as she gasps, her eyes widening as if she's surprised herself at the speed with which she responded.

She starts to say my name, but the pleasure's either too intense or she's determined not to give me what I want, so I pump harder, deeper, nipping at her neck until she comes again, and this time, my name spills out in a fierce cry.

"Harrison," she practically screams, her voice echoing throughout the barn. "Oh God, Harrison."

My own orgasm spills out, shaking my entire body, ricocheting through every part of me as I lose myself inside of her. I breathe hard against Emery's neck, giving myself another moment to be here, to be so close and forget, for a moment, that this was a hate fuck, the last hate fuck.

The last time I'll hear her post-orgasmic breathing as she comes down off this spectacular high.

CHAPTER ELEVEN

EMERY

MY BODY'S STILL VIBRATING, recovering from my orgasm when Harrison pulls back from me, nearly dropping me on the ground as he turns away to grab his pants. It's so unlike him that it shakes me more than the sex just did, making me blink at his sculpted back as I try to find the words and collect my thoughts.

"What the hell was that?" I ask, pulling a few strands of hay off my underwear so I can slide them back on.

He doesn't answer. He just keeps looking for his own clothes and pulling them on, so fast that he's back in his stupid city clothes within moments. Buttoning his shirt, he turns to look at me. His eyes are cold again, like they were at the farmers' market, and it seems impossible that just minutes ago he was inside of me.

It felt so… I hate to say it, but it felt perfect. With Harrison, it always feels perfect. Even a freaking quickie in the barn feels special. Maybe it's the fact that he's the only man I've ever slept with because it seems impossible that this moment should always feel so charged.

Clearly, Harrison doesn't feel the same way.

He's still watching me, measuring out his answer to my

question. I watch as he licks his lips, knowing he must taste our kiss.

"What was that?" I ask again, wishing that I didn't feel like crying.

I know that, whatever answer he says, I'm not going to like it.

Not with the way he's looking at me.

He holds my gaze as he says, "Closure."

My heart shatters. I knew I wouldn't like it, but there it is, the word hanging in the air between us. A word that means the end of this. The end of us.

When he kissed me, I thought he'd decided to try again. I'd hoped that this was his way of rekindling. That no man would fly from New York to Kansas just to return an old hoodie or whatever it is that I left behind.

That he was ready to try again.

I was stupid, obviously. This was his way of closing the book, of putting one last romp through the sheets—or, I guess, through the hay—in as our last chapter. He doesn't care about me. He probably... God, I already forgot we're not exclusive. He probably banged Claire before he got on his stupid jet for his closure fuck with me.

Gross.

How could I be such a fool?

Still, even with my heart in tatters, I have to recognize this as an opportunity. If Harrison's closing the book on us, then I need to say my piece. I have to leave it all on the table so I don't think about all the things I didn't say forever.

"Fine," I say, forcing my voice not to shake. "Then there's something I need to tell you."

He watches me. Nearby, the horses neigh and paw at the ground. Probably the ones I haven't fed yet, protesting. But they'll have to wait.

"I'm sorry," I say, not knowing how to begin.

Harrison doesn't look impressed. "Sorry for what? For screwing me over or for just plain screwing me?"

"I'm sorry I agreed to do what Blythe wanted," I say. "She paid me to date you. I admit it. It was terrible. But she…she told me you were a horrible person. She told me you wouldn't let her go. That you wouldn't sign the divorce papers and she just wanted out so badly. And well, she told me lots of things that weren't true."

Harrison just stares at me, completely blank faced. I'm not sure if he doesn't believe me, or if he just doesn't care.

"And you believed her?"

"I don't know what to believe," I snap back, thinking of Claire.

God, does Harrison look at her the way he used to look at me? Does he give her two orgasms in a row? Does he make her feel like she's the only woman in the world for him? That no one else could ever measure up?

I push those thoughts aside. Blythe may have lied about a few things, but clearly, she was right about some things. Harrison's cold, an asshole, only here because he wants to control the narrative of our breakup. He can't stand that I left New York before he was ready for me to go. Before he got his closure. And he's just rich enough and stubborn enough to come all this way to rub that in my face.

"But I'm also sorry for catching feelings for you," I say, anger flooding my voice. "I never dreamed I would. And I shouldn't have, obviously. But I gave the money back, Harrison. I didn't go through with the deal."

A flash of something in his eyes, but it might just be the light from the barn. He doesn't say a word.

But this isn't for him, is it? This is me clearing the table, the slate, the whatever. If I'm going to go back to my old life, I need to eliminate Harrison completely. I need to tell him the whole truth and be done with it.

"And I guess I'm even more sorry that I can't seem to

shake these feelings, even after it's over," I say. "Especially since you've made it clear that you're a rotten apple anyway."

His lip twitches slightly at that. Memories of the lawyer? Laughter at my pathetic apple joke? Or…something else?

I don't get the chance to decipher it. Harrison slides his shoes onto his feet—they're filthy, thanks to the barn, at least —and turns around, leaving me alone in the barn, particles of dust floating in the afternoon light. At the sound of his car starting, I walk over to the barn door, watching as his car pulls away from our driveway.

Watching that car, listening to the gravel crunch beneath his departing tires, I decide I feel lighter. Better. I did what I needed to do. I said what I needed to say. Hell, I'm not even crying about it.

Or I guess I'm only crying a little. Just a tear. A tear's allowed in a moment like this, right?

I return to the horses, swiping the tears off my face. I focus on Brownie, my favorite horse, the one I grew up with. As I lean against her, she nudges me with her velvet nose.

When the tears continue to come, I try to tell myself that it's not Harrison. It's everything else, the moving and being back here. Nostalgia and regret.

Not Harrison. Anything but him.

Then Brownie nudges me again, this time at my overalls pocket. I reach inside and pull out a bit of apple, and that's when the sobs start for real.

Because who am I kidding?

It's all about Harrison.

And with my luck, it always will be.

CHAPTER TWELVE

HARRISON

SHE ADMITTED IT.

She dated me because Blythe paid her to.

She took Blythe's money to manipulate me.

Or she meant to take the money, but at the last moment, she experienced…what? Regret?

I can't spend my time dissecting why Emery decided to give back the money. In fact, I know what I need to do. I need to call Sandy, tell her to book my pilot for a return to New York, and move on. After all, I've had my theories confirmed out of Emery's own mouth. I got her side of the story, didn't I? And I even got the hate fuck I wanted.

Mission accomplished.

So why the fuck am I still in this godforsaken town looking for a place to stay?

Unfortunately, there aren't any five star hotels here, at least not anywhere in a hundred mile radius. There also aren't any Marriotts or Hiltons or even so much as a Holiday Inn. There is, however, internet. Thank God for that, I suppose.

There's an inn.

One.

And I can tell from the outside that this place hasn't heard of thread counts above two hundred. I also suspect this is more of a bed-and-breakfast than an actual hotel. If this ends with me renting a room with a shared hallway bathroom—

It doesn't even bare thinking.

Still, it's getting dark, and I'm running out of options if I'm going to stick around in this place for another night. And that must be what I need. Just a night to get some clarity. Not that I plan to see Emery again. No, that's definitely off the table. But maybe just being here will give me the answers I need. Some sort of closure-by-proximity or something. And it's a really long drive back to the airport.

I reluctantly park and head inside. It'd be just my luck that they're sold out tonight. The perfect ending to this idiotic trip to the farm. I give in to a fit of whimsy and imagine myself sleeping in a barn tonight before shaking my head, smiling despite myself. I'd sleep in my car first.

A grey-haired woman wearing a sweater that she definitely made herself greets me at the front. She smiles and whistles when she sees me.

"Well, what do you know!" she says, her name tag declaring that her name is Annie. "You look like you stepped right out of a magazine, handsome."

I offer a smile. "You don't have a vacancy, do you?"

"As a matter of fact, I most certainly do," Annie says, beaming. "I've got one guesthouse left. Busy weekend," she adds.

I laugh. It's genuine. The woman's earnestness wins me over. Also the fact that she'd refer to anything in this town as busy. Still, the mention of a guesthouse sounds promising. If I can get out of this trip without sharing a bathroom, it'll be a real win.

"Fantastic." I smile back at her, already reaching for my wallet. "I'll take it."

"Only one problem," she replies, because of course, there's a problem. "It's the church."

"Excuse me?"

"The guesthouse we have left, is the church. It sleeps six and it's our most expensive guesthouse."

I blink.

"It's a converted church!" she adds quickly at my blank look. "Converted into one of our guesthouses! I can get you in at three hundred a night, but if you're staying more than two nights we can move you over to one of the cabins for one fifty a night." She beams with her offer of accommodations. "Wi-Fi's free," she adds when I don't respond.

"I'll take it," I finally say, placing my credit card on the countertop.

"How many nights?"

"I'm not sure yet," I say, though I should tell her it's just one. I don't know what the hell I'm doing.

"We'll just put in a week, but it's fine if you need to make it less or more," she says, and then she squints. "Is it 'fewer' or 'less'? My daughter's the sixth grade teacher, and she's always harping on me about that."

Not "a" sixth grade teacher, I notice. She's "the" sixth grade teacher because this town is so small that that's a possible distinction, apparently.

"You need any advice on the sights to see?" Annie asks, typing away into her ancient desktop computer. "We've got some real hidden gems."

"Not right now, but I'll keep the offer in mind," I say.

"Well you let me know," she says. "And we've got church on Sunday. Whole town makes it out. It's a real event." Then as if it's just occurred to her that she needs to clarify she adds with a delighted laugh, "Not the church you're staying at, of course."

She grins as she passes me my key. Not a piece of plastic but a real, actual key.

"Now, you shouldn't have any trouble finding the old church," she says. "We've only got five guesthouses, all on the same street here. The old church is four doors to the left. Number '7' Pearl Street. Can't miss it."

"Thank you," I say. "I appreciate your hospitality."

She beams at the compliment. "Aren't you sweet. Need a wake-up call or anything, Mister…"

She glances at my credit card. "Mr. Duke?"

I wait for the recognition of my name, but it never comes. She just blinks happily in my direction.

I take the card. "No, but thank you."

She smiles. "Have a wonderful evening, Mr. Duke."

Returning to my car I grab my Rimowa from the trunk and drag it over the uneven sidewalk. The wheels squeak a bit in protest when it hits the ground, as if it, too, isn't thrilled to be spending the night in Cottonwood Falls, Kansas. Hell, my suitcase cost more than the most expensive room in town.

I find the old church easily, seeing as I can see it from my car. Annie's right. Four doors to the left. I'm still a little incredulous at the idea of spending the night in a church, but here I am. It's a tiny, old stone building. I turn the key in the classic old wooden door, stepping into a surprisingly modern space inside.

Granted, my expectations were low.

Beamed ceilings and hardwood floors. An open kitchen, a couple of bedrooms behind it. The furniture and the linens look like they must have been trendy back in 2005, but now, the glossy wood bedframe and the maroon bedspread with gold tassels looks, well. Dated's a kind word, I guess.

Still, it looks clean, and the towels are neatly folded in the bathroom with a little handmade soap on the top. I know it's handmade because there's a card next to it that says, "Made with love by local farmers right here in town!" I wonder if Emery's family is responsible for this soap, but I push the thought from my mind.

Emery's family. Emery's town. She grew up here in this sleepy place. The most excitement outside my window is a couple of trees swaying in the breeze. Beyond that, it's fields and dirt and more fields and dirt.

I understand now, Emery's fascination with New York. Like it was the shiniest, most fascinating place to ever exist. New York is nonstop bustle compared with most cities, but compared with Cottonwood Falls? Night and day.

I turn the water on in the shower, which groans before producing the most aggressive spray of water that I've ever seen. It practically sears my skin off, and I end up battling with the showerhead for a good five minutes before I get it to produce water at a reasonable pace and volume. Then, once it's hot, I step into the standard tub-shower-combo. It's not the luxury walk-in I have at home, but at least the handmade soap smells decent. Like lavender, I'd guess.

With the warm water spraying across my back, I think about today. About Emery and her confession.

I don't know what to do with it. The words simmer in my mind, rolling over again and again. The last part, in particular, sticks in my mind.

She didn't want to "catch feelings"—what a phrase—but she did. And she regretted them because she thinks I'm an asshole who was fucking Claire the entire time.

I wanted her to think that. I needed her to know she didn't win as she was counting her money. But apparently there wasn't any money, since she never cashed the check.

Does that make what she did forgivable? My ego growls in response. Of course it fucking doesn't. Emery might have started as an innocent virgin, but even innocent virgins know better than to play with someone's feelings. With their fucking heart.

And then there's the fact that I don't even know if I believe her confession. How would I know if she really had feelings for me? I think of her writhing against me, moaning my name, and my dick hardens. But that's just lust.

Isn't it?

My traitorous brain remembers quieter times. The way she listened as I told her about Robert and Blythe. The secrets she shared about her parents' divorce and about her brother. The way she genuinely wanted to help my business—me —succeed.

Would she have done any of that if she was just in it for career advancement or fucking?

I don't enjoy any of these thoughts. In fact, I'd like nothing more than to push them aside, including the ones that sparked the hard, throbbing cock currently erect in the shower.

Suddenly, the water turns cold. Apparently, showers at the Pearl Street Guesthouses can't handle more than twenty minutes.

Whatever. I welcome the cold. It's exactly the reality check I need.

I towel off and head to bed, though I'm unfortunately correct about the thread count. Apparently, luxury brands have not made their way to Cottonwood Falls.

But whatever. This is fine.

I fall asleep, telling myself not to think of Emery and thinking only, of course, of her.

CHAPTER THIRTEEN

EMERY

I WAKE UP FEELING LIBERATED. Harrison Duke is out of my life, and I'm free to do whatever I want.

Heck, I'm free to do *whomever* I want. I am no longer a sweet little farm-girl virgin. I am an experienced seductress of the city, currently thrust back in Kansas but definitely enjoying it, and I can do whatever I want.

Yes, I'm definitely feeling liberated. Not miserable. Nope, not at all. I have an entire day to do chores around the farm. And who cares if they're the same chores that I did when I was a teenager and it feels a lot like regressing? Who cares that my college degree is a complete, irrelevant, waste when it comes to chores? Not me.

No, I'm invigorated. I'm full of purpose and drive. Towards what, it's still unclear. But I am going to do something today. Something that puts me on track to success in my future.

Mom's watching me suspiciously as I aggressively stab my eggs and wolf them down like an underfed dog. She's always wanted me to be a "daintier" eater, but apparently, I'm even more violent than usual this morning.

"Calm down, hon," she says. "You know they're already cooked, right? No life in them."

"I'm just hungry," I say.

"I bet," she says. "Bet you've been working up an appetite with all your…chores."

For a second, I freeze. Did she somehow hear about what I got up to in the barn yesterday? She didn't get home until hours later, so I know there's no way she actually heard anything. But could a neighbor have heard? We don't have anyone nearby for miles.

"It's been an adjustment," I say, hoping I'm just being paranoid for no reason. The gym in New York is no match for farm chores. "But I'll get back in the swing of things. You can take the girl out of Kansas, but you can't take Kansas outta the girl."

Mom smiles. "It's nice to hear you say that."

I don't tell her that the words feel empty. Besides, the more I say it, the more I'll believe it.

"I thought I'd get a ride in," I say. "It was nice with Candace the other day."

"Always a good way to start the day," Mom says. "After your chores, of course."

How is it that, a few weeks ago, Mom was able to get through these chores without me? I want to tell her I'm not sixteen anymore, but then I stop myself because I'm being a brat. Here I am, staying here rent-free, for who knows how long, knowing she struggles…and I'm resenting her.

"Of course, Mom," I say. "After my chores."

The chores themselves don't take long. I clean out the barn, throw in fresh hay for the horses, check on the chickens, and work through the rest of the list. It's hot out today, and I'm glad I threw on my trusty Daisy Dukes. I found them battered at the bottom of a dresser drawer, but they fit like a glove. A tight, somewhat short glove, but still.

I also dug out an old T-shirt from high school, one so short that it doesn't even attempt to reach my hip bones. How the hell I was wearing this on a regular basis is beyond me, but the old cotton's comfortable, so I wore it.

The heat continues to beat down on me as I work, reminding me that this is another part of Kansas I've apparently lost my ability to deal with. New York's heat was different, smoldering somehow. Something you had to suffer through in your air conditioned office. But here...well, here I can actually do something about the heat.

I abandon my riding plans and jog down the gravel road away from our house until I get to a fork in the road. It leads me to a bridge and a place that I spent way, way too much time at during my teenage years. It's the Cottonwood Falls River, a slow, sparkling oasis that's just begging for me to dive in.

And why the hell shouldn't I? A little river swim might be just the baptism I need for moving on to the next phase of my life.

The water's steady and clear, and I find my favorite place to wade in after tossing my boots off. The mud's slippery and squishy under my toes, the water the kind of cold that scatters all of my thoughts. I grin and then dive right in, clothes and all, letting the water cool and cleanse me all at once.

It's beautiful here. Birds chirping, leaves rustling, a horn honking...

Wait, a horn honking?

I pop up out of the water and look at the bridge. There's a car parked there, and I squint to try to make out the driver. Then, a car door opens and closes, and a man appears, walking with a smile so smug that I think it should be illegal.

"Does this qualify as a public pool in Kansas?" Harrison asks me, his sunglasses glinting in the sun. "Looks nice."

I throw back my wet hair, trying to scrounge up a witty comeback. None jumps to me, unfortunately.

"It certainly is," I say instead. "Want to join me?"

Why, why am I doing this? Harrison made it perfectly clear yesterday that we are over, done, kaput.

But then again, he's here. On my bridge by my scrap of river.

Harrison gestures to his clothing. Another sport-coat-slack-combo not suitable for the country. I find myself wondering if he packed ties out of habit. "I'm not dressed for it," he says.

"So what?" I say, splashing the water with my hand. "I'm pretty sure you once told me that it didn't matter if you got your clothes a little dirty. You said you had money to burn."

He chuckles. "I won't come in, but let me get down there."

I watch as he pulls the car to the side of the road and then heads down the path to meet me. I relish that he and his ridiculously expensive shoes struggle a little on some of the rocks. It's not easy to throw Harrison Duke off his game, but apparently, Mother Nature is up to the task.

After he finally gets to the bottom and next to the bank, he looks at me as if to say, what the hell now? And because I've apparently lost my entire mind, I splash him.

You know.

Like a child prankster.

He stares at me. "What are you doing?"

"I don't know," I say. "What are *you* doing? I thought you were done with me. Or is this part of the closure process?"

I'm baiting him, but I don't care. Because he's here, and even if he is a nonexclusive asshole, he's here, and my mind can't process anything else.

He doesn't have an answer, and I decide to make things just a little more difficult for him.

I swim to the edge of the bank where he is and stand, the water making my already tight shirt and shorts cling to my skin. I can feel that my nipples are already hard beneath the wet fabric, and whether it's from the cool river water or Harrison, I don't know. But I do know that his eyes drop to them, and his mouth opens. I'd bet anything he's hard as hell for me right now.

"What did you say?" Harrison asks, dragging his gaze from my tits to my face with difficulty.

"I asked if this was a step in the closure process," I repeat. "I don't know how this works, after all. I've never closured with anyone before you."

He smirks, reaching out to cup my chin. "Well then maybe I'd better show you."

CHAPTER FOURTEEN

HARRISON

I DIDN'T EXPECT to find Emery like this. I thought I'd drive by her place, take a final look, and then head to the airport. It's what I decided when I woke up this morning, still thinking about her and her damn confession.

Only, as I neared her house, I saw her running along the road. She'd turned off the path and onto the bridge. And so I followed to see where she would go.

I didn't expect her to jump right into the water, clothes and all. And though I should have expected her to emerge from the water in a wet shirt—due to her jumping in with her clothes on and all—I wasn't expecting to be so swayed by the sight of her in a wet T-shirt clinging to her tits. She'd braided her hair into two braids, and all I thought about was how I'd like to pull them as I fucked her from behind.

And I sure as hell didn't expect her to get all sassy with her line about not having closured with anyone before me.

It's those words that make the decision for me. Before I can think of a response, I've swept her up in my arms, and her mouth's on mine, kissing me with the same ravenous hunger as before. I turn, dropping onto a soft patch of grass and lay her back on it, kissing down her jaw and then her neck as she shivers.

"I hope this suit isn't dry clean only," she says, nodding to where my shirt and jacket are now soaking from holding her against me, but sounding anything but sorry.

I rip off the jacket as I kneel above her.

"Guess you'll have to get creative about paying me back," I say.

She doesn't waste any time, sitting up to reach for my belt as she yanks my pants down, revealing my hard cock. It's right there at her mouth level, and she crawls forward on hands and knees, taking a tentative lick along the shaft that makes me groan.

She casts a hungry look up at me before moving forward and capturing the tip in her mouth, sucking eagerly as she swirls her tongue around the head. Her mouth's warm, and I shudder in pleasure.

"You're a filthy girl now, aren't you, Kansas?" I ask, loving how her eyes widen as she continues to suck me deeper and deeper into her mouth.

She pops my cock out of her mouth and runs a finger along the edge until she gets to my balls, cupping them in her soft hands.

"Only because you made me one," she says.

If there was any blood left in me, it rushes to my cock, making it throb harder. It misses her mouth, and I thrust my hips back toward her lips. She licks again, capturing the pre-cum with the tip of her tongue. She swallows it before wrapping those lips on me again, and I nearly lose it all at just the motion. At just those words.

Only because you made me one.

I pull back from her, and she looks up at me with worry or irritation, I'm not sure which, but I pull her up and capture her mouth in mine and she moans before I can determine if she's worried or annoyed. I need her, need more of her, so I ease her back against the grass. Within seconds, I've stripped her of her wet clothes and have yanked off my own. I stare down at her naked body and all its beautiful curves. I trace kisses from her jaw to her neck to her breasts, loving the sharp inhale of breath she gives as I reach one of her nipples. I flick the tender skin with my tongue before pulling the whole thing into my mouth, and she moans, arching her hips forward.

She wants me. Wants me here on the fucking grass beside a stream, and like hell if I'm not going to give it to her.

I kiss my way down, further and further along her stomach as she squirms beneath me. Her legs part slightly as I reach the sensitive skin of her thighs, and I tease her with kisses that move closer and closer to that fantastic pussy of hers. I can already tell she's going to be slick with want for me, and I'm dying to taste her.

But first, I want her to beg me.

I move closer still, running my tongue just an inch or two from where she really wants it as she clenches her thighs. And then, just as it seems like I'll give her a proper lick, I move back up again to kiss at her hipbone.

"You horrible, horrible man," she says, her voice nearly a low hiss. "What the fuck are you doing?"

I look up at her, flushed pink with lust for me. And I smile.

"Tell me what you want," I say. "Beg for it."

She groans in frustration, and I run my tongue along her hipbone as she bucks again into the air.

"I want your mouth on me," she says. "Fuck, I want it so badly Harrison that I could scream."

The words burn inside of me, and I drop back to her pussy, running my tongue along the folds before diving inside, tasting her sweetness as I flatten and lick as she writhes against me. I find her clit and swirl my tongue there, sucking and teasing, relishing how her breaths come hard and fast.

Her orgasm shakes through her, and she cries out with pleasure, her thighs shaking around me. I rise up from her, grinning at my ability to undo her so easily.

"Emery, I need to be inside of you," I tell her, watching as she pants.

"Yes," she agrees. "Yes, please, yes, Harrison."

I pull a condom from my wallet and slide it on quickly, teasing her pussy with a finger as I do. With it on, I watch as she parts her legs wider, giving me the hottest view I've ever seen. I move forward and position myself at her entrance, pulling her legs up a bit off the ground as I thrust into her.

She moans into me, but then I remember the braids. Fuck, I want to pull those braids.

I flip her from her back to her stomach and yank her up to her knees then drive back into her. She squeals at the sensation, and then those squeals turn into whimpers and cries of pleasure as I drive deeper into her from behind. Her ass is smooth and full against me as I thrust into her.

But it's not enough. I want more. More of her, closer than ever. So, I pull her up so that she's sitting up on her knees with me behind her, gliding in and out of her as she pants.

"Feels—so—fucking—good," she whispers, and I agree.

I bite my lip and grab one of those braids, giving it a tug. She grins back at me in response, eyes full of lust.

"You like that?" I ask.

"Hell yeah," she says.

I grab the other and pull, shifting her forward a little as I pull on her hair and fuck her hard from behind. She pushes back against me, too, both of us rocking together, until she comes again, and I come with her, both of us drowning in pleasure. In each other.

After, we fall back against the grass, and she rolls over until her head's resting on my chest.

"I guess I like closure," she says with a smile. "At least, if this is what closure's like."

I smirk. "I think I do, too, Kansas."

"How long does closure last though?" she questions, staring at me under impossibly long lashes.

"Another day maybe?"

She considers it, then after a moment, counter offers. "Maybe a few more days?"

"Maybe a few more," I agree.

CHAPTER FIFTEEN

EMERY

IF THIS IS what closure feels like, then yes, I can do this for a long, long time.

After we both recover from our orgasms, I take another quick dip in the river, though Harrison refuses to. I watch him from the water as he puts his pants and shirt back on, though he folds the suit jacket over his arm. I don't blame him, not in this heat.

"Where are you staying?" I ask him, bobbing in the water.

"At one of the Pearl Street Guesthouses," he says. "You know it?"

I nod. "There's only one place in town, really. But it's nice."

Harrison snorts, and I roll my eyes.

"Okay, fine, it's not a five star hotel or anything..."

"Emery," Harrison says. "It's not even a hotel."

I giggle. Just the thought of billionaire Harrison Duke at one of the Pearl Street Guesthouses is ridiculous. Staying in a room the size of one of his closets, probably.

"Hey, don't talk shit about the Pearl Street Guesthouses," I tell him. "The sweetest couple runs it. They also sell at the farmers' market. Doug and—"

"Annie," Harrison finishes. "We've met. She's very invested in me going to church today. That is, if I'm still here."

If he's still here. Just the mention of it, the reminder that he is, in fact, still here in my tiny Kansas town.

But not for long, apparently.

Why is he here, though? I think about asking him, but then I decide not to. I don't want to spook him and scare him away.

"So, are you going to go?" I ask tentatively. "To church, I mean."

He stares at me, not the blank way from the other day, but the way he does when he's considering whether or not a business deal is worth the effort.

Am I the business deal in this moment? I mean, I know I'm not a business deal like that. Like what I—sigh—almost used him for. But am I someone he's deciding whether or not to invest in? Is he weighing my worth against other women? Claire, maybe? Hell, I think he's still technically married… Does he compare me to Blythe?

"I told Annie that I was planning to leave," he says.

"Oh," I say, deflating a little.

"But my plans appear to have changed," he says. "At least, for the moment."

That makes me sit up in the water. I'm still naked, and I can feel his eyes on me in that hungry way again.

Closure.

But also, plans for church.

Maybe I need to put my clothes back on.

"Turn around," I tell him. "I need to get out of the water."

He raises an eyebrow. "You're not serious."

"Yes, I most definitely am," I say. "I can't talk about church while I'm naked."

"I didn't realize we were still talking about it."

"Just…just turn around, okay?"

He rolls his eyes but turns around. I dash out of the river and pull on my clothes, which have thankfully dried a little in the hot sun.

"Okay," I say. "I'm ready to talk about church."

He peeks over his shoulder and then, seeing that I'm dressed, turns all the way around.

"I didn't realize it required more discussion," he says. "Even if I'm staying, it doesn't mean I'm going to take Annie up on her offer to go to church. I thought we might spend more time in that barn of yours. You know, doing the closure."

I bite my lip. "Well, it's just that…it's not just Annie's church. My family goes, too. It's less religious and more… well, more social. My mom uses it as an opportunity to parade me around."

He considers this. "And you want me to be part of the parade?"

Would this conversation be so hard if he was still my boyfriend? And hell, was he ever my boyfriend? We didn't really get around to labels like that. I never got to have the thrill of telling my mom, hey, here's my very successful, very handsome, very New York boyfriend. And I definitely don't get to say that now. What would I say?

Mom, here's the man I'm in an emotionally complicated, purely sexual relationship with. I've decided he should come to church with us?

My mom wants me to find a man, but even she wouldn't be thrilled about that.

"No," I say at last. "I don't. But I also don't want to go alone. It's sort of, um. Awkward. Being back."

We're treading into dangerous territory. Feelings territory. And even though I've never closured anyone before, it feels like, if we're going to keep doing what we've done twice now, feelings need to be off the table.

"But you grew up here," Harrison says. "You have… friends here. Don't you want to see them?"

I can tell he's thinking about Pete. I can't help but laugh. Sure, I've got Candace, but Pete? There's nothing Pete and I have to talk about. Not anything interesting, anyway.

No, I don't have friends here. I barely had the chance to really make friends in New York. Not besides Harrison.

"I do. But I could use the buffer, you know? Someone who can help me deflect all the questions about New York," I say. "So I don't have to face it all alone."

"And how would I say that I know you?"

I close my eyes. It's like he's reading my mind. He knows I can't call him my boyfriend. Not even my ex.

"How about my friend?" I ask. "Would that be okay? Just until…until this closure's done?"

He thinks on this. I can already hear the word "no" falling from his lips. He's going to say no, of course. It's a ridiculous ask.

"Yeah, fine," he says at last. "I could do that. For a day."

It'll be enough, I decide. Enough for now.

———

MOM PRACTICALLY HITS the roof when I tell her that I'll be bringing a guy to church. She spends the rest of the morning asking me questions, and when I tell her it's my friend from New York, she gets even more curious. I don't tell her that it's Harrison, though. I tell her his name's Gary and that we worked together. And that—God help me—he's just passing through town. No one passes through Cottonwood Falls. Not on purpose, anyway. I don't like lying to my mom, but I also don't need her giving Harrison the side-eye the second she sees him. She doesn't know everything that happened, but she knows enough. Calling him "Gary" is safer.

"Well, I'm guessing he's more than a friend," she says for

the billionth time over toast before we head off to church. "Friends don't just pass through Cottonwood Falls for a quick visit, you know."

I bite my cheek to keep from answering and nod instead. Because what she said is true. Friends don't do that. But egotistical billionaires who apparently aren't done messing with your mind and who look insanely hot in suits and who you would give anything to have look at you like they trust you again?

Yeah, those guys will fly over to see you.

Though why they might stay…that's another story.

I meant what I said to Harrison about church being more about the social aspect. It's why I'm dreading it already. I'm in a pale pink dress with shoes that pinch at the back because they're small on me. I feel like a cupcake, but it's not like I can wear jeans to this. Or overalls. Or short shorts.

I braid my hair and twirl it up into a bun, and then I put on some light pink lipstick and eyeliner. It's the most done-up I've been since I landed in Kansas, but it's nothing compared to Mom. She's got on her full face of makeup, a pale green dress, and her hair curled and pinned back. She looks gorgeous, and I wonder if it's because she's meeting "Gary" or if she's maybe got her eye on someone at church.

I don't have a chance to ask, though, because soon we're rushing out the door and picking up Candace before landing at the dusty steps of the church that baptized me. I recognize the pastor who looks older every day but still has a twinkle in his eye. I look for Harrison as we take our seats but don't see him, and I wonder if he's bailing. If he decided to hop on that private jet and get the hell out of Kansas, after all.

"Honey, don't worry," Mom says, picking up on my anxiety. "He'll be here. And if he's not, then—"

"Is this seat taken?"

I nearly jump at the sound of his voice, and I whip around to find him standing next to me, smiling. This isn't the brooding expression he's worn with me for the past couple of days. This is the warm, charming Harrison Duke smile, reserved for clients he's wooing. There's a deeper smile, a more sincere one, that he used to use only for me, but I don't think I'll see it again.

Even so, Mom lets out a squeal and bounces out of her seat, grabbing his hand and giving it a firm shake.

"Harrison Duke," she says. "It's a pleasure to meet you."

Harrison... what? How the hell did she know it was him? I thought I told her it was Gary—

"You look just like your pictures online," Mom says, still shaking his hand as he beams at her. "I was hoping you'd come."

She flashes me a meaningful look.

What the hell? How did Mom figure me out? How did she know he'd be here? And why isn't she furious at him? Is this an overdose of Kansas kill-them-with-kindness?

But I don't get to ask because the pastor's taking his spot at the front. Harrison settles in on my left with Mom on my right. He's so sturdy next to me, and I suck in a breath and smell his cologne. Musky and rich and delicious, just like the rest of him.

Not the thing to be focusing on in church.

Luckily, I'm distracted by the return of all of the old church rituals. It's not that I expected to forget in a matter of months. But it's just like everything else in the town. Nothing changes.

Nothing except me.

The second the service wraps up, every family in town seems to descend on us. Whether they're drawn by the new man or my stories of New York, I don't know. But within seconds, there's a flurry of questions, comments, and, oh yes, plenty of concern.

"Honey, you look so grown-up. New York must have done a number on you. But we're here for you, obviously."

"Still pretty as a button. I've got just the dress for you in my shop. You come on by, and we'll give you the special."

"I read that awful article that was going around about subway crime in New York. How anyone stands it, I surely don't know. We're glad to have you back, darling."

"What a brilliant young woman you are, landing a job in a big New York City office. Though I don't blame you for scooting on back. They can't possibly make pie like we do in New York, can they?"

It's sweet, all of it, and sweeter still that Harrison manages to smile through it all. But I'm prickly. I feel the way they're wrapping around me with their words, trying to drag me back into the fold. But standing here, with Harrison, I realize that it's not just him I missed. It's New York.

Being home feels like a failure. Like I gave up, and I guess I did. I want to be back there, and it hurts to even think it.

"I don't know if I agree about the pie," Harrison says to one of the biddies with a chuckle. "I have a baker in Brooklyn who'd beg to differ."

This ignites a flurry of other questions, mostly about what New York is like, and I step back a bit, letting them encircle him as he grins and smiles and plays along.

Candace appears at my side. She watches the scene with a soft smile and takes my hand, giving it a squeeze.

"You told Mom, didn't you?" I ask. "About Harrison coming to church."

Candace shrugs. "She asked me. And she asked if we should be mad."

"And what'd you say? I thought we decided he was an asshole."

Candace stares ahead, watching as Harrison gets a big laugh from the crowd. Something about pecans, I think, being part of superior pie.

"I think he might be an asshole," she says. "But I also think that he's here, and I think that you two have a lot to work out. And…well, I also think something else, but I don't think I should say."

I glance at her. "That's not fair."

She turns and grins at me. "I think it's something you'll need to figure out for yourself."

I roll my eyes, knowing I won't get a better answer from her. So I watch Harrison and how easily he smiles. I watch him and worry that this is all an act, one that threatens to disappear at any second.

"Candace," I say. "Why is he here?"

She looks at me, eyes shining.

"You know why he's here, Em," she says, squeezing my hand again. "He's here because of you."

CHAPTER SIXTEEN

HARRISON

I SHOULD NOT STILL BE in Kansas.

I should be on my plane heading back to New York.

I should not be talking casseroles with Emery's mom in her kitchen that looks like it was pulled straight out of a sitcom on country living.

And yet, here I am.

"Casserole is, far and away, the most efficient and most delicious food on God's green earth," Emery's mom argues. "It's just delicious."

I laugh. "With all due respect, ma'am, I've never been a casserole fan. Call it the New York in me."

Emery's mom purses her lips in a way that so reminds me of Emery that it makes something inside of me twist.

"Well, I'll just have to accept that you haven't had the right kind of casserole," she says. "But don't worry. We'll fix that."

I chuckle. I don't tell her that yesterday, after church, I tried at least four casseroles that were forced upon me by various middle-aged women at the after-church social. There's no need to offend her.

Besides the casserole overload, though, I'm finding that I

don't despise Kansas as much as I thought I would. Sure, the Pearl Street Guesthouses continues to be motel quality—nice, but—and I feel like it's impossible to get all of the dirt off of me at the end of the day in that pathetic excuse for a shower, but otherwise, it's not completely without merit.

The weather's a nice break. Nature's refreshing.

And then, of course, there's Emery.

I catch a glimpse of her through the kitchen window. She's chatting with a neighbor who "stopped by"—or, more likely, heard there was an out of towner at the Mills place and purposefully drove here. Emery's smiling and chatting, offering her jars of jam. She's in a little apron since she was just here in the kitchen, helping her mom with the latest batches of strawberry basil and apple.

"She's a special girl," Mrs. Mills says behind me, and I catch her watching me watching Emery.

I clear my throat. "She is."

She nods, gaze sweeping across the room and into the living area. There are pictures of Emery everywhere, as a baby crawling across the carpet, as a kid riding a pony, as a teen with a pointed graduation cap.

"What are the two of you doing, anyway?" Mrs. Mills asks, and I choke on the sweet tea I'd just taken a sip of.

"Pardon?"

"Oh, Mr. Duke, don't be so obtuse," she says, waving a hand. "Emery told me you two were having some trouble. But I can't help but see how you look at her, and, well, a woman my age knows a thing or two."

A woman her age. I don't bother reminding her that she's not that old. Especially not considering the age difference between Emery and me.

"You make her happy," she says simply. "Even when you're annoying the shit out of her."

I stare at her, at this woman who is alternately sweet and strong. Her eyes flash as she turns a spoon in her simmering pot of jam, and she looks to the front door as it jingles with Emery appearing there in the frame.

"Well, it only took two jars, but Mrs. P's gone for now," she says. "Though I'm sure someone else will show up any second."

She laughs, turning to me. Her smile falters a little. It never used to do that. She used to look at me and let her smile light up her entire face.

But now, it falters.

Because of me.

Because I can't forgive her for what she did.

Unless…

"You know the county fair's today, baby," Mrs. Mills says innocently from the stove. "That might be a good place to hide out, you know."

"Oh, sure," she says. "I'm sure that's just where Harrison wants to spend his time. The county fair."

"Well, it's got to be better than sitting in our kitchen watching you cook," her mom counters, pointing a spoon at her. "Now, go on and clean up. I'm sure Harrison and you'll have a great time."

"Mom…" Emery says, looking desperately to me.

Her confession rings in my memory. She took a business deal, and that deal involved dating me.

Who am I to judge, honestly? I look around at the kitchen, including the stack of bills pinned to the fridge, and realize that Emery and I are not of the same world. And she took an opportunity. A bad one, in my opinion. But she took it.

And then she, as she said, "caught feelings."

And she never took the money.

Fuck, it's so clear that I'm the asshole here. So clear, especially with her mother watching me, waiting for me to fix this. It's spelled out plainly on her face.

You make her happy.

Yes, I sure as hell do. And I intend to make her even happier.

"I'd love to go to the county fair," I say. "If you're up for it."

Her mouth falls open, and I smirk.

I think, the only thing I enjoy more than Emery Mills, is surprising Emery Mills.

———

THE COUNTY fair is held out in a series of open fields, and it's the quintessential county fair, or so Emery tells me. There's a Ferris wheel and plenty of stands with different games, and the whole place smells like caramel and popcorn.

"We really don't need to be here," she says for the tenth time. "I appreciate you playing along to make my mom happy, but—"

"Emery," I stop her, grabbing her hand. The touch sparks between us, and her eyes widen. This is the first time since New York that I've touched her without the intent of sleeping with her.

"I'm happy to be here," I tell her, and it's the truth. Aside from one call to Ramon to let him know that I'd be unavailable for the next few days, I haven't thought about work since I landed in Kansas. I've only thought of one thing. One person.

Emery.

"You don't have to say that," she says, looking away from me.

"I'm saying it because it's true," I say.

Suddenly, horrifyingly, her eyes water. They glisten in the sharp, blinking lights of the fair. We're walking along the edge, and no one notices, but still. I don't need to be known as the asshole who made her cry.

And more than that, I don't want her to cry. Not here. Not ever.

"Then why are you here?" she asks, voice breaking. "Are you just trying to torture me when you say stuff like that? Is it some kind of weird payback? Because that…that doesn't feel like closure, Harrison."

It's true. It doesn't sound like closure.

Because, I realize, I don't want anything less than I want closure.

I want a new beginning.

"I found the check," I tell her. "I thought you'd been playing me. I thought it was all fake."

"But I told you it wasn't," she snaps.

"You told me here," I say. "Not in New York."

"You didn't give me a chance!" she says, eyes flashing. "I tried, Harrison, I wanted to talk to you that night but you got called away. Then the next day I tried talking to you but weren't interested in hearing anything I had to say. You were very busy with…with that lawyer."

Now, the tears fall down her cheeks, and I step closer to stop one with my fingertip.

"Don't," she says, shaking her head, but she doesn't pull away.

I tip her chin up so that she can look at me.

"It was a lie," I say. "I wasn't with Claire. I just wanted to hurt you the way you'd hurt me."

Her eyes widen in realization. "You lied?"

"And I'm sorry I did," I say. "Honestly. But you should know, there's nothing between Claire and me." I pause thinking that statement through. If we're being honest, I don't want to restart with a lie. "There was at one time. Nothing serious," I hasten to add at the flash of ire on Emery's face. "But not since I met you."

"Well," she says, stepping back, "you can't do that! You can't fake-bang a lawyer every time you get mad at me!"

I laugh. "I can promise that, Kansas."

She smiles and then breaks out into laughter with me. I reach out and take her hand again, pulling her close to me.

When her lips meet mine, fireworks in the sky light up.

Even the county fair seems to agree with the moment.

CHAPTER SEVENTEEN

EMERY

I SPEND the rest of the county fair in a haze of joy.

He wasn't with Claire.

He doesn't *want* to be with Claire.

He wants to be with me.

He wants to be with me at the county fair, arguably the dorkiest place possible for a man like Harrison Duke to be.

He takes it in stride, though. He tries five different fried foods and declares that fried ice cream is delicious but fried turkey legs are disgusting. He plays an entire row of games and wins me three stuffed animals that I end up giving to a group of kids who look on enviously. When he sees this, he wins another one for me to take home.

We ride the Ferris wheel like we're in a movie, and when we're at the top, he kisses me, and it's soft and wanting and passionate.

And romantic. That too.

And God, I want him. I want him so badly that I'm practically vibrating. I want to feel his skin against mine. I want to feel him inside of me knowing that I have him, I have him, I have him.

And judging on the look in his eyes, he wants me, too.

"I have an idea," I tell him once we step off the Ferris wheel.

A very naughty idea.

The Maguire family barn is really, really close to the edge of the county fair.

They sometimes use it as an event space—it's a popular venue for country chic weddings—but with the county fair happening right around the corner, I know it'll be vacant. And as soon as we get there, I'm proven right.

I look at it and then look back at him with my best wicked grin.

"You told me you wanted more closure in the barn, right?"

He closes the distance between us, snaking a finger along my jawline.

"No more closure," he says. "But an empty barn, Kansas? Hell yeah."

His lips are on mine in a second. I manage to maneuver us around the corner from the doorway, just in case anyone else wanders this way, and then I let him hoist me up as I wrap my legs around his waist, feeling the hard press of his abs against my bare thighs.

I changed into a dress before we left, a sundress with the kind of straps that require you *not* to wear a bra even if you wanted to. Harrison pushes down the front until he frees my breasts, taking one into his mouth as he holds me up.

God, that man and his mouth. The heat and slick pressure of his tongue sends a shiver through me, wetness and heat pooling between my legs at his touch.

He swirls his tongue around my breast, giving a final nip of the tender peak before he sets me down just long enough for us to strip off our clothes like we're in a race. His fantastic cock springing from his clothes and into the air. I take the hard, throbbing flesh in my hand and fist around it, feeling how heavy it is in my hand.

"You're perfect," I tell him, and he groans in response.

Dropping to my knees I wrap my lips around his cock, watching as his head falls back, mouth open with pleasure. Pleasure that I'm giving him as I move my mouth up and down his shaft. The sight of him so undone by me drives more wetness between my legs, and all I want is him inside of me now.

I roll my tongue in circles over his cock, pulling back as I examine the glistening, hard flesh. Then, I stand, watching as he levels his eyes on me.

"One second," I tell him, grabbing a chair from a nearby table, one meant for a reception or a baby shower or some unknown innocent purpose. "I want to be on top of you," I tell him, and then I kiss him, deep and hard as I push him to sit and grind my pussy against his shaft, shivering at the feel of him so close to me.

"Let me get the condom, you little sex imp," he says, but he's laughing.

I pout a little as he moves away from me, digging into his pants as he plucks the condom out of a pocket.

"You're always prepared," I tease him.

"With you, I have to be," he tells me. "You're insatiable, obviously. Attacking me in every random barn we pass." Then he winks and God, I love that. It sparks even more want inside of me, and my whole body feels electric with want.

The condom slides easily over his cock, and he sits again. He even has the audacity to put his arms behind his head.

"What are you doing?" I ask him.

"Oh, I think I'm going to enjoy the hell out of this ride," he says. "Now, hop on up."

I get back into my position straddling him, angling his condom slick cock between my legs. I feel him there at my entrance, so big and hard, and then I guide the tip inside of me.

And oh.

Oh God.

He slides in as I sit down, feeling him so deep inside of me, angled so that muscles I didn't realize existed begin to clench. My pussy clamps around him, and I rock forward and gasp.

"Oh...oh my God," I murmur, shocked by the intensity.

Harrison's hands come down and he grips my ass, guiding my pace as I move forward and back, feeling the curve of him inside of me.

The orgasm builds quickly inside of me with sharp spikes that come with each rock. I want to go faster, faster, chasing the height of my climax, but Harrison's hands move me slowly, and I bite my lip as sparks of pleasure build and burn inside of me.

Then, it's too much, and the orgasm spills forward as I scream and straighten, and he comes, too, arching deeper inside of me as he thrusts one final time.

I collapse against him, both of us breathing hard. He turns his head and kisses my jaw, and when I open my eyes, he's looking at me like I'm the most beautiful woman he's ever seen. Like there is no comparison, not here in Kansas or New York or anywhere.

And then he smiles, that smile that's just for me.

And I know, when he does, that I am completely and totally his.

CHAPTER EIGHTEEN

HARRISON

IT'S the look in her eyes, even when she thinks I'm not looking at her. She watches me like something special to be protected. And not that I need protection. But it's a good feeling. She doesn't look at me like she has an agenda. She never did, really. She doesn't look at me like I'm something she can use to get ahead.

She wants to have me, just as I want to have her.

We head out to the grassy hill next to the barn and lay on our backs to look up at the stars blinking in the sky. It's so pure, so Kansas, so Emery, that I can't help but be there with it. I don't think I've ever had such a pure moment in my life. Especially not mere moments after one of the hottest moments of my life back in the barn.

Soon, though, there won't be any more Kansas stars above me. No casserole—though I'm much less upset about that. I'll be back in New York because, although the vacation's been nice, work will need me eventually. I do have a company to run, after all.

I look at Emery. The idea of returning to New York without her, though, unnerves me. I'd gotten so used to her being there in my office and my home, like it was meant to be that way. And now, with this week behind us, I know that she belongs there with me.

But does she feel the same way?

"You know, this might ruin my Kansas cred, but I think I miss a good bed," she says, plucking a strand of grass out of her hair as she rolls on her side to look at me."

"Oh?" I ask, hoping she's thinking along the same lines as me. "Any bed in particular?"

She laughs and rolls her eyes. "Oh, I dunno. Yours was nice. Not as nice as your kitchen, but fairly decent, I suppose."

"I knew it," I say. "You're sleeping with me for my kitchen."

"Don't be ridiculous," she laughs. "I'm sleeping with you because you're good in bed. Your kitchen was just a bonus."

Was. Was a bonus.

She smiles. This is fantasy talk, but it's hitting close to home regarding what I really need to know. So I might as well just come out and ask, right?

But what if she says no? Fuck, I'm turning into a teenager again, worried she won't want to go to prom with me. Of course, it's more serious than that. I'd be asking her to uproot her life. And hasn't she already uprooted it once, anyway?

And though she won't say it, I know this place doesn't feel right to her. She said as much before church.

She leans back, gaze returning to the stars. "Do I make you happy, Harrison?"

"Yes," I say, not giving the question a second thought. Because it's true, dammit.

"Really?"

I turn to her and smile. "Emery, you make me happier than I knew was possible."

She kisses me again, her lips pillowy soft against mine. I pull her closer, tasting her, feeling her arch against me under the starlight. I run a hand down her body, relishing her shiver as she throws back her head.

My hands dip under her dress, tracing circles on her thighs.

"Again?" she whispers against me.

I shake my head. "Just for you. You deserve it, after all of that riding."

She giggles, but it turns to a moan quickly as I press my fingertips against the thin fabric of her panties. I can feel she's still slick beneath them, and my finger slides under easily. I tease her pussy, running gentle traces along her lips, and she shivers and bucks her hips forward.

I roll her onto her other side so that my chest is flush against her back, continuing my ministrations with my hand as I kiss her neck just beneath her ear. She gasps, and I continue to kiss as I add a second finger, pumping slowly inside of her, feeling her tighten around my hand.

"I love how you feel," I tell her, and she pants, grinding against my hand, urging me to go faster.

I comply, fucking her with my fingers, continuing to kiss her neck and swirl my tongue across her shoulders. My cock hardens against her back, and I press the hard flesh against her so that she knows how endless my want for her is.

But even so, I make my cock wait. I focus on her, on the feel of her, on finding just the right places. She's become a lock that I am just the key for, and her body answers mine with every motion. She takes me and takes me, beautiful and glistening with lust in the starlight. I keep going, moving my thumb in circles against her clit, until at last my name tumbles from her lips and she comes hard against my hand.

She's still panting, eyes unfocused, when I capture her mouth in another kiss. She returns it earnestly, just as in need of me as I am of her.

I pull back and see her eyes sparkling at me.

"Come back with me," I say. "To New York."

Those little doe eyes widen to epic proportions, and she pulls back, her lips slick from our kiss.

I suppose it's unfair of me to take advantage of her in her post-orgasmic glow, but all's fair when you're trying to get what you want.

Or something like that.

"What?" She blinks at me like she's not sure she understands what I'm asking.

"Just say yes," I instruct. "I know you want to."

"It's not that easy," she says, sitting bolt upright. "I can't. I have no money, no apartment, no job…"

I fail to see the problem here.

"I have money," I remind her. "And an apartment, and an entire company at my disposal."

She looks at me, her eyes momentarily suspicious.

"You also have a wife."

I sigh. She needs to understand. Whatever happened before with my feelings about the divorce, none of them matter anymore. And I made my decision, and I meant it. I wasn't lying to her before.

"I signed the papers."

"Because I tricked you into it," she objects, flopping back onto the grass.

"No, because it was long past time that I did." Long past time. If anything I'm grateful for the nudge into making it official because what I have with Emery is nothing in comparison to anything I ever had with Blythe. Even with our unconventionally weird start.

"Really?" she asks. "It's over?"

I nod. "It's over, and all I want is for you to be there with me. So say yes, Emery. Say yes and we'll leave tomorrow."

She stares at me, silent for a long moment. An impossibly long moment.

Then, with a smile, she says, "Yes."

CHAPTER NINETEEN

EMERY

HE'S NOT MARRIED ANYMORE. He's a free man. No, not just a free man.

He's *my* man.

I'm still riding a high when I get back to the barn. Harrison left to go get his stuff and check out of his rental, leaving me some time to pack up my own things. I can't even believe this is happening. I hadn't even wanted to dream about the possibility that Harrison would consider taking me back and forgiving me for everything that happened with Blythe, and now…now all he wants is me. He wants me. And he wants me with him in New York.

My grin's threatening to reach epic proportions as I do a ridiculous spin as if I'm filming a scene in *The Sound of Music* or something. Laughing, I lean against one of the saddles. The smell of leather fills my nostrils, and I hear the sounds of the horses whinnying. It breaks me temporarily from my thoughts about New York, reminding me that, before I leave, I've got goodbyes to make.

I walk over to Brownie's stall and find her watching me. She walks up to the gate, and I let myself in. Immediately, she tucks her head in against my shoulder, like she's a dog waiting to be pet. Of all the horses I grew up with, Brownie and Jackson were my favorites. Brownie though, always felt like she knew me. She flicks her tail, those huge eyes watching me with a steady gaze. I run my hand along her velvet nose, and she leans into my touch.

"You know, don't you?" I ask her, and I swear she actually nods. "You know I'm leaving again."

I lean against her warm, round stomach. She was one of the good parts of being back home. One of the steady parts.

"I'm glad I got to see you," I tell her, and I can't believe that I'm actually tearing up. "I'll be back soon. I promise. To visit. And I'll...I'll make sure that Mom doesn't skimp on the carrots. I'll make sure she's taken care of, too. That's all I ever wanted. To make sure she's okay. And you guys too, obviously."

I'm rambling, but Brownie doesn't care. She just keeps her nose pressed against me, nickering occasionally. Now, I'm not just kind of tearing up. I'm crying, soft little tears that slip down my cheeks. Brownie rubs one of them away with her nose.

"I messed up before," I say. "But I'm not going to do that again. Whatever happens, I'm moving forward. I'm going to make my life happen."

"Messing up's part of the journey, hon. Don't you be ashamed of it."

I turn, and there's Mom, standing there in her beat-up jeans and fraying straw hat. She's smiling at me, big and warm. She walks over, looking at me and Brownie with the same kind of love she looked at us with when I was a kid just learning how to ride and barely tall enough to brush Brownie afterwards without help.

"Mom—"

"I figured I was on borrowed time with you, baby," she says. "And I'm excited for you. He's *so* handsome."

I have to roll my eyes. Of course Mom's forgiving me for leaving again because I'm leaving with a handsome man.

"It's not just him," I say, which is true. "He's a big reason. But...being home made me realize I'm not done with New York. And I don't think New York's done with me, either."

Mom steps into the stall and gives me a hug. Brownie nudges her shoulder, and Mom laughs. I see that I'm not the only one tearing up around here, but she smiles and pulls back.

"Look at you nosey little thing," Mom says, patting Brownie. "You can have your tearful goodbye but I can't?"

Brownie snorts in response, and we both laugh.

"We're going to miss you," Mom says. "But I'm glad you've found your path. And you know I'll always be there to support you."

I smile. "I'm supposed to be the one helping you. You know that's one of the reasons I left, and I intend to make everything right. I don't want you to have to worry about anything. Harrison—"

"I appreciate that," Mom says. "But I don't want you focusing on me. You've got a big journey ahead, and I can't wait to see what you do with it."

Now, the tears really come. She pulls me into another hug, and Brownie and Jackson paw the ground and whinny. It's a proper Kansas goodbye with the dust stirring up in the light, and hope fills me up from the inside out.

"Now come on inside," Mom says, pulling back and wiping her own happy tears while I swipe at my own. "We've got some packing to do, and fast. I'm pretty sure I just heard that man of yours pull up."

I nod. "Yeah, he's got his own plane so I think he's ready to head to the airport."

Mom starts. "He owns a plane? Well baby, I'm more than happy you've bagged this man. Because with a private jet, you don't have any excuses not to visit anymore."

I laugh, and we hug again one more time. Then, Mom troops off in her boots, and I give Brownie a last kiss on her cheek, just under her eye.

"I'll be back," I promise. "But you take care of everything while I'm gone, okay?"

Then, I slip her an apple from my pocket, and she munches on it happily while I say goodbye to Jackson, then leave the barn. I know they understand. Like Mom, I know the horses love me and want me to be happy, whatever happens next.

Harrison helps me pack up my suitcase, but it honestly doesn't take very long. It's kind of sad. I did leave most of everything I owned in my apartment, after all. I didn't think I'd need it again.

And now...

Now, I'm starting from scratch. Again.

Harrison suggested I can stay with him but moving in? So soon? And I don't even have a job.

Shit. I know that New York is the right answer, but now that I'm thinking about it, I'm going to really have to hit the ground running. Mom's right that I have a journey ahead of me, but one thing's for sure. I'm definitely missing a map.

Harrison's hand touches my shoulder, and I turn to see him looking at me. God, the way he looks at me. Like I'm the best thing he's ever seen. Like I'm the most perfect thing on the planet, even though he's *seen* all of the most beautiful things—and people—on the planet.

But none of those matter.

Not compared to me.

He pulls me forward, and I fall against his chest, let his lips capture mine in a kiss.

"I'm glad you're coming back with me," he says. "It hasn't felt right without you."

And then, all of my worries, all of my fears just evaporate. Because I can make anything work as long as I have this man by my side. As long as he keeps looking at me like that.

Oh, but maybe not like *that*, I think. Because his eyes have dipped down to my cropped shirt, and that hunger from earlier is sneaking back in.

"Harrison," I scold. "My mom's in the other room. And don't we have a plane to catch?"

He smirks. "It's my plane. It doesn't matter what time we get there."

"Still," I say. "Being prompt is important, you know."

He laughs. "You're right. We can just fuck on the plane."

Heat rushes up and down my spine in an instant, and it takes every part of me not to throw him back on my twin bed and have my way with him.

Thankfully, I hear Mom banging around in the kitchen, and I remember exactly why I can't do that. I also remember another reason I'll be glad for New York.

Privacy.

And sheets that feel like butter.

A shower that fits two people.

And so, so much more.

"Let's hurry," I say. "Everything wrapped up at Pearl Street?"

He nods. "I broke poor Annie's heart by checking out. But I told her I'd be back."

I smile at him. "Now she'll be bragging to everyone about her celebrity occupant."

He catches my mouth for another kiss. "I'd hope so, Kansas."

"You're going to have to come up with a new nickname," I say. "Now that I'm moving back."

He shakes his head. "It'll always be Kansas for me. That, and Coffee Girl. Though it seems like you've moved beyond both of those."

I think of my time here with Harrison, memories of the

barn and the grass as he kissed me and pressed our bodies together. Maybe I know myself better because of it, and for that, I'm glad.

"Let's go home," I tell him. "You and me, New York here we come."

CHAPTER TWENTY

HARRISON

SHE SAID YES.

She's coming back with me to New York and…well, thank fuck for that. I hadn't realized how badly I needed her to say yes until she'd paused before agreeing. Or more accurately, I knew exactly how badly I needed her to say yes and when she'd hesitated, I hadn't liked it.

To say the least.

Looking at her now, I can't believe my luck. Both in finding her and in getting her back.

We say goodbye to her mom—who makes me promise to make ample use of the jet for Emery to visit—and then Emery says a final goodbye to the horses.

"You can come back whenever you want," I tell her. "I meant what I said to your mom. Anything you want, it's yours."

She smiles, glancing at me from the passenger seat of the rental car as I drive us to the airport. The hundred and fifty miles aren't nearly as annoying with Emery beside me. She's giddy, nearly as excited as I am to be going back to New York. Or maybe more. I'm just going home. She's returning to a place she was still learning and falling in love with. A place she never should've left in the first place.

Thinking about it, though, I'm glad I came to Kansas. I might not miss the church converted into a makeshift hotel, but Kansas gave me some much needed clear air and perspective. A clear head about Emery and everything else. It also gave me the opportunity to see where Emery grew up and meet some of her family. I know it meant something to her, which makes a week-long trip to a place I'd normally fly over well worth it in the end.

Now, it's back to reality. Duke Capital's gotten by this week without me, and even if there weren't any major fires, I'll have a lot of catching up to do. But hell, I'm playing catch up even when I'm in the office. And now that my divorce is finalized, I'm also going to need to figure out what, exactly, to do with Blythe. I don't want her staying on at the company, and I know I need to clean up the mess that she's made of the charity department, but I'll need to be diplomatic. Unemotional. That's something I'll need to ask Ramon about, especially since, now that Emery and I are together, remaining diplomatic about my ex is going to be a tough tightrope to walk.

I wonder what Blythe will think when she finds out Emery and I are together. Really together, and not together due to her shady manipulation. But for once, I don't find the same bitter resentment coursing through me at the thought of Blythe. For one, I know that Claire will have made sure that Blythe didn't get everything she wanted.

And I know that she didn't get the one thing she wanted: me, heartbroken and devastated. In fact, I'm quite opposite.

I should write the woman a thank-you note. It might be petty, but it'd be satisfying as hell.

"What's so funny?" Emery asks, eyebrow raised.

"Nothing," I say. "Just excited to get home."

"Me too," she says. "I've already texted my old roomies. I think we're going to go out for Thai food."

I glance at her. "Really? Aren't you worried you'll be a little jet-lagged?"

She waves that off. "No way! I can sleep on the plane."

"I'm not sure you're going to do much sleeping," I say suggestively, raising an eyebrow.

She laughs and swats at me. "You are insatiable, you know that?"

"Just making up for lost time."

"It wasn't *that* much time," she insists.

But it was. Every minute that I wasn't with her was a waste, and I intend to make up for it. Something that will be difficult if she's already filling up her social calendar with her friends.

Of course, I want her to spend time with her friends. There's nothing wrong with it. I just didn't realize it would be happening so soon.

"Anyway, they say there's a cute place, and I've missed New York food. And restaurants open past eight, honestly."

"That, I am in full agreement with."

"Besides, I know you probably have to start catching up on work," she says. "Was this your first vacation in like five years?"

"No," I say.

"Conferences don't count."

"Then yes."

She laughs. "Well, that's going to change. Now that I have you, really have you, we're taking time off together. We could spend an entire week playing tourist! I still haven't seen the Statue of Liberty, I mean not up close anyway. We could do a tour of cupcake shops. The observation deck at the Empire State Building. Rockefeller Center at Christmas. We'll walk the Brooklyn Bridge in spring. Eat somewhere uber trendy in Park Slope. A picnic in Central Park over the summer—"

I can't help it, I laugh. We're about to board a private plane and she's planning all of our travel in the city we live in.

"We can go anywhere, you know," I offer, imagining all the places I'd love to whisk her away to. If she loves the energy of New York she'd swoon over Tokyo. She'd be charmed by London and enchanted with Paris. I want to see the world all over again through her eyes.

Hell, when did she turn me into such a damn sap?

"Anywhere you want," she replies with an easy smile, sinking back into her seat as she looks out of the window. The airport is in sight now, the sky littered with planes at various stages of take-off and landing.

"Anywhere *you* want," I counter with a grin of my own.

Starting, of course, with New York.

Before we know it, we're up in the air in the jet. And as soon as we're at cruising altitude, Emery can't resist a quick lie down in the bedroom.

Nor, it would appear, that she can resist me.

CHAPTER TWENTY-ONE

EMERY

BY THE TIME we land in New York and make it back to Harrison's apartment, I hate to admit it, but I *am* a little tired. Ugh. I hate when that man is right. Or more correctly, I just hate it when I'm wrong. Then again, I don't mind the reasons why I'm tired. And sore. And completely and totally satisfied.

Still, a promise is a promise, and I do want to see my old roommates, especially because Harrison said they were pretty harsh on him when he saw them, and I'd rather tell my side in person. I'm also simply thrumming with possibility and excitement. I'm here! Back in the city that never sleeps, which is honestly thrilling because all Kansas does is sleep.

Haha, not really. Mom wouldn't stand for that kind of slander against Kansas.

But one thing about New York? Places are open late. Past eight, past ten, even! And they make more than just burgers and casseroles. They even make Thai, which I've been craving ever since Sherri suggested it. Yes, one growl of my stomach tells me that I want Thai food. Like, right now.

I take a peek at Harrison. He's in the sitting area of his bedroom, because you know his bedroom has an actual sitting area. For what I don't know. There's an actual living area, and a den in this monstrosity of an apartment. I wonder if the architect designed the space for an impatient man waiting on his partner to finish getting ready. Harrison's not waiting for me though, nor is he impatient. He's kicked off his shoes and is already sipping a whiskey, his laptop flipped open as he scrolls through what I can only guess is a total deluge of emails. It's clear he'll be wrapped up in that for the night.

Was he working while he was in Kansas? I have to imagine he hit a bit of a productivity wall. Between the motel's undoubtedly shitty Wi-Fi and our barn escapades... there wasn't a ton of time for work.

Work.

A job.

Which reminds me that I still have my whole life plan to figure out. I run my fingers along the clothes I've pulled out of my suitcase and hung up in his closet. Or our closet? I don't even know. But somehow, just being in this closet makes my clothes feel fancier. I grin and pull out one of my favorite dresses, a fit and flare navy one that shows off my calves. Then, I take a quick shower to clean off any last bits of travel off of me. I pull the dress on, and then I look in the mirror.

A girl, born and bred in Kansas, but *made* for New York. I'll make sure of it.

But first, I need to tend to my empty stomach.

"Okay, I'm heading out!" I chirp to Harrison as I walk over and kiss him. He tastes like whiskey, and he grabs my hand to keep me from spinning out of his grasp. I giggle, and he deepens the kiss.

"So you're still going?"

Is he pouting? How adorable.

"Yes, I promised my friends," I say. "But don't worry. I'll

be back later, and then you can have your filthy way with me."

He smirks. "Do you need me to call Leo?"

I shake my head, checking that I've got everything in my purse.

"It's just right around the corner. I'll see you later."

I kiss him again, relishing the taste and feel of him. I only barely manage to pull myself away before I get too tied up.

Then, with a wink, I'm out of the door and taking the elevator to the lobby before a doorman hastens to open the door for me. The New York night air's cool, making me glad I grabbed a coat. Everything about this city feels busy, and I love the energy.

The place that Sherri picked is in Hell's Kitchen, so I hop on the subway to get there. It's not a long ride, but I love every minute of the people watching. Hell, nowhere else in the world has people watching like New York. And people watching on the subway is practically a requirement. I could read, sure. But people watching is both entertaining and safer, right? I make sure I don't look creepy while I do it, doing my best to be subtle while my eyes rove from the couples snuggled against each other to the eccentric artists sketching in their notebooks to the people in their suits back from a late night of work. Everyone in New York has a story, and I just desperately want to be part of it.

And sure, I suppose a subway ride isn't exactly around the corner, but where I'm from, three miles is absolutely right around the corner.

Exiting the subway, I climb the stairs back to the street and walk to the restaurant to find Sherri and the rest of my former roomies waiting outside. They see me walking up and squeal, immediately pulling me into a hug. There's a new girl there, and even she joins in the hug. They pepper me with comments as they smother me.

"I can't believe you came back."

"We missed you so much!"

"Do you want your stuff back?"

I laugh. "I'm happy to be back. And no, you can keep it. I don't need it."

"But where are you staying?" Sherri asks, quirking an eyebrow. "Not with the asshole?"

"I promise, he's not an asshole," I say. "But I'll tell you everything just as soon as I have some drunken noodles in front of me, okay?"

That elicits a few "ohmygods" and "tell us everything" responses, but I refuse to say more without food. We head inside and order basically everything on the menu, sharing spring rolls and stories as I get them up to speed.

"Wait a minute," Sherri interrupts my storytelling. "He actually showed up in Kansas? I know I was harsh on the guy, but wow. Props."

"That's just the beginning," I say, and then I really spill. As much as I feel comfortable with, leaving out the finer details of our barn escapades. At one point, I get out my phone to show some photos from the county fair, and that's when I see a series of missed texts and calls from Harrison. I also see the time. How did three hours fly by that fast?

But we're almost done. I'll call him back in a bit once we're finished.

"One question," Sherri quips, leaning back as she drinks a Thai iced tea. "Did he land the private jet in a cornfield or what?"

I laugh. "You're such a farm-ist, Sherri. First of all, you can't land a plane in a cornfield. Second of all, he had to land at an airport in Kansas City. Then he drove a very ordinary rental car to Cottonwood Falls."

"I'd do basically anything for a private jet," Dana, one of my other roommates, interjects. "Like, anything. Obscene things."

"I'm not with him for the jet," I say. "I swear. I'm *falling* for him. Crazy bad."

They "aww" around the table, and I don't even try to hide my blush.

"Well, what're you going to do now?" Sherri asks. "You're staying with him, and then what?"

"I am," I say. "And then… I'm not really sure. I need to look for a job."

"Do you really have to, though? I mean, you're dating Harrison Duke. You're not splitting the rent and he can literally buy you whatever."

I nearly laugh out loud at the idea of splitting the rent on Harrison's place. I couldn't afford to split the utility bills on that apartment. I shake off the absurdity of Harrison's life and answer.

"I want to work," I say. "I just don't know exactly where yet. But I want my own income, even if it's irrelevant."

"Exactly," Sherri says. "You're an independent woman. You can want a man, but you don't *need* him."

Except that, right now, I kind of do. Unless I make some changes. And fast.

The rest of dinner wraps up fairly quickly, and I promise to keep in touch and get together again soon. I'm buzzing off the conversation and friendship—and some of the wine I had, honestly—as I hop on the subway for my return trip. I try to call Harrison, but my phone's battery completely gave up on me during dinner. I've got a useless brick in my hand. Oops. I probably should've charged it after the flight.

But whatever. I'm almost home, and then I can tell him all about my night in person, which is more fun anyway. We could, for example, be naked while we talk. Absolutely more fun.

The silence and the rocking of the subway gives me space to think, too, about what my friends said. About being my own person. My mom basically said the same thing as well. And I want that. I want to find my own path.

My own yellow brick road as it were. I'm not in Kansas anymore, which is definitely the first step. Now how the hell do I find the right path?

CHAPTER TWENTY-TWO

HARRISON

WHERE THE HELL IS EMERY?

I'm annoyed—and something far worse: worried—looking at the flurry of text messages that I've sent to her over the last several hours, all of them unanswered and staring back at me. My thoughts run wild; something terrible has happened to her, a mugger or worse. But I tell myself to calm down. She wouldn't have gone to anywhere unsafe, would she? She knows better.

Then again, does she? She's been living in that tiny town for most of her life, and even after she moved here, she didn't know New York the way true New Yorkers do. Hell, she fucking smiled at strangers all the damn time. She'd talk to anyone. Jesus.

What if she smiled at the wrong person? Caught the wrong creep's attention?

But she was with people, I remind myself. Her old roommates, friends. Just around the corner, she'd said. How much risk could she be in within a block or two of my apartment?

In New York? Plenty.

And then, of course, there's the other part of me, a part I don't like much, that feels like this is a little too familiar.

That remembers Emery looking at her phone, her eyes flickering across text messages as she laughs and turns the phone over.

Because that was what Blythe was doing. Every late night that she was unreachable was a night that she was wrapped up in another man's arms. And even though I know that Emery isn't Blythe, something about it all burns hot within me.

I just got her back. I just got her back in my life *and* New York, a city that she was clearly pining for. The *life* that she was pining for. And did I ask for anything in return?

No, though apparently, I should've asked for a fucking response to my messages.

I'm pacing, about to call Leo or Bruce to go out looking for her. Because something must be wrong, this late at night, for her to not even answer a single text. What kind of wrong... I won't think about it.

Except, we're good, me and her. She's got no reason to be ignoring me. Hell, we just made up for Christ's sake. So the only reason for her to drop off the grid like this...isn't one I care to dwell on.

I've grabbed my jacket and am about to dial Leo's number when suddenly keys jingle in the door, and relief and fury slam into me simultaneously at the sight of her.

Her hair's come out of the little updo she'd pinned it up into, and her skin's tinged pink from the cold night air. Her lipstick's faded, but she's smiling at me like absolutely nothing in the world is wrong.

"Oh Harrison," she says, tugging off her coat and tossing it on the rack by the door. "I've just had the most magical night. You were right. This *is* where I want to be. And now that I'm here—"

"Where were you?" I say, forcing my voice to stay level. "I texted and called you, and you never answered."

She blinks, taken off guard. "Oh, right. I lost service on the subway, and then my phone died after I got to the restaurant."

I stare at her. "You took the subway?"

She waves me off, taking the stairs up to the bedrooms as I trail behind her. "Of course I did. I wasn't going to walk that far! Besides, it was good to be on it again. Felt like I was really back in New York, you know?"

She takes off her earrings, dropping them onto the dresser. I watch as she does, fists curling at my sides as I tell myself to breathe. To not lose it on her.

"Emery," I say. "That was dangerous. You can't be taking the subway this late."

"This late?" she laughs, casting me a bewildered look. "Harrison, it's 10:30."

"Eleven," I correct. "And that is late. Too late for the subway. I have a car service on standby whenever Leo isn't available. You'll use them from now on."

She laughs again, and then she turns her head and sees that I'm not joking. Her smile falters and her eyes widen.

"You're not serious, are you? I told you, my phone died. It's not that big a deal. I did it all the time before."

"And you shouldn't have done it then," I say. "You don't understand this city. If you're going to live here, you need to be safe."

"You're not really going to tell me that," she says. "Harrison, I'm an *adult*. I know how to take care of myself."

"It doesn't seem like it. Not if you're going to do this kind of shit."

"This kind of shit?" She narrows her eyes. "I took the subway, Harrison. Calm down. Do you think you're going to tell me what I'm allowed to do?"

"No," I reply as calmly as possible. "But I will do whatever it takes to protect you. Even when you insist on acting like you're still in Farmville."

"Are you sure this is about me?" she asks, putting a hand

on her hip. "Taking the freaking subway? Or is it about you being paranoid and jealous?"

I rankle at that. "Don't—"

"I'm not her, Harrison," she says, the words slicing through the air. "I'm never going to do that to you. And I need you to trust me."

She closes the remaining distance between us, her eyes blazing right in front of me.

"I'm yours," she says. "But I can't spend the rest of my life apologizing for our very weird beginning. For taking a shady job from your ex before I even knew you. I will never cheat on you. And I will never lie to you again. But I need you to trust me, okay?"

I do trust her. And I don't think she'd ever act like Blythe, even if that was one of the things that made tonight triggering. It's more than that. How can she not see that this is a world that would want to take her and harm her? How can she be so goddamn naive?

Being with me makes her a target of sorts. I keep a relatively low profile, so the risk is low. But still. With great wealth comes increased threat. Now that we're public, the threat extends to her.

She looks at everything with joy and optimism, never thinking that anyone or anything might hurt her. Never imagining that there are people out there who would hurt her while she looks at a ride on the subway like it's the fucking Magic School Bus.

But I can't say any of that. Not without making her regret being here with me. Not without ruining more of the world for her. I'll just have to protect her my own way.

Her hands touch my face, drawing me back from my thoughts.

"All I did tonight was brag about you," she says, smiling. "I could not shut up about how amazing you are. About how there's nowhere in the world I'd rather be than right here with you."

She drops her hands, sighing as she steps back from me.

"We also talked about how I don't know what I'm doing with my life," she says. "Which remains a mystery, unfortunately."

I take her hand. "You'll do whatever you want."

There's no need for her to be worried about that. With the amount of money I have, she has all the time in the world to decide what her long-term goals are.

Because right now? Looking at her in that dress, I know exactly what my short-term plans are.

I take her hands to my lips and kiss them. She looks up at me and smiles, arching an eyebrow.

"I thought you might be too tired," she teases.

"For this?" I say, kissing her knuckles and relishing how she shivers. "Never."

I pull her against me, and she responds by burying her hands in my hair, each of us desperate for more of the other. My cock hardens against her, and she lets out a little gasp as I grind it against her leg. She moves to take off my shirt, and I unzip and yank her dress up and over her head. With her tits freed, bouncing in a lacy bra, I move her back against the wall, pressing her against the unforgiving surface while I continue to grind my cock against her. She arches her back, and I pick her up by her ass, kneading the soft flesh with my hands as she wraps her legs around me. Through my sweatpants, I can feel the heat of her pussy against me, the way she wants me. The way she needs me.

I turn and carry her to the bed, nipping her neck as I go. As I toss her onto the mattress, want and desire course through me. She lays there on her back, propped up by her elbows, eyes dark and dilated, lips parted and glistening from our kiss. She spreads her legs for me, her pussy flush and swollen and waiting for me to fuck her.

I grab a condom and shrug off my sweats and boxers, letting my hard cock spring into the air between us. She runs her tongue along her lips at the sight of it, and I smirk.

"I want you in my mouth," she tells me.

"Too bad," I tell her. "I want it somewhere else."

She grins at that, and I love how naughty she is for me. How dirty she's become.

I roll the condom on. She moves to sit up, but I'm there before she can. She gasps as my body crashes against her, my cock pressed against her clit as I push her back further on the bed. She angles her hips up and rocks them, her head tilting back as she all but vibrates with pleasure. I ease two fingers into her, feeling how slick that tight little pussy of hers is for me. She cries out, her body jolting back, but I grab her with my free hand and hold her steady as I fuck her with my hand. She moans at the sensation, relaxing into me, her pussy growing wetter and wetter with every thrust of my fingers.

Then, standing, I grab her ankles with both hands, yanking her to the edge of the bed where I stand, cock lined up precisely at her entrance.

"Tell me you want me," I say, staring into her eyes as she stares right back into mine.

"Yes, I want you," she says. "Now, Harrison. Now, now—"

With a single drive, I'm inside of her. I'm pumping my cock into her sweet little pussy, and she's moaning and gasping as I do. Her breathing quickens, and I watch as she rolls her hips in rhythm, taking more and more of me deeper inside of her. I hold her in place with my hands on her ass, gripping the supple flesh tight so that I can work my cock deeper into her.

I only release her to grab her hand and place it on her clit, moving her hand under mine in circles. I watch as her eyes roll back at the feeling, as she pants and plays with herself. Her hips buck against me until her orgasm crashes through her, making her even wetter as her cunt tightens and convulses around my dick.

My own orgasm follows, a rumble of curse words tearing out of me as I drive into her. Fuck me, it's perfect. She's perfect.

She's mine, she's mine, she's mine, and that more than anything is what pushes me completely over the edge.

CHAPTER TWENTY-THREE

EMERY

TODAY IS A NEW DAY. A new day for me to figure out what the hell I'm going to do with my life. Because no matter what Harrison says, I can't live off of him. I'm far too young to be a trophy girlfriend. Err, well I'm probably exactly the correct age to be a trophy girlfriend. But that's not what I want. I want to make my own way, figure out my own path. Something about New York speaks to me, and I just need to figure out what it's telling me to find and where to find it.

First start, a job of my own.

I pull out my planner and find the page that I'd made with a list of my dream jobs before I moved here the first time. There's a list of around twenty, but there at the top, decorated with stars and different colored ink, is the internship for Duke Capital. Next to it, in cursive letters is my written declaration that, "I did it! I landed the job!"

My heart sinks a little. Duke Capital was my dream job. And the work that I was doing with the Pink account... It really felt like I was close to finding my path. If I hadn't detonated my life like a bomb.

But I can't just blame myself. There was Blythe. I'd love to be furious at her, and I am. Then again, without her interference, would I have started dating Harrison? It's hard to say.

Actually, it's not that hard. The answer is no. I'd have scurried around the office avoiding eye contact with him at every possible opportunity because I'm kind of a wimp, femme fatale wise. I'd never have dared to so much as flirt with Harrison without encouragement from his wife.

Ugh, that will never not be messed up.

Still, score one for karma. Can you imagine hiring someone to flirt with your spouse for the soul purpose of getting them to sign off on a divorce and instead she falls, really and truly, head over heels for him?

Ouch.

All of that is beside the point, though. The point is, I need to find a job, and I'd love to go back to Duke Capital. Would they take me? It wasn't like I was fired. Sure, I did quit my internship early, but perhaps I'm rehirable? I think Ramon might be willing to put in a good word for me, and he might even give me a recommendation. I could ask Harrison, of course, but he'd just wave a magic wand and give me a position I don't deserve or say I don't need a job at all.

No. I'm doing this on my own.

I scour the website to find open jobs at Duke Capital that I'm qualified for, then I edit my résumé and cover letter and fire it off to HR. When I'm done with that I draft a quick email to Ramon asking if he can possibly provide a recommendation or at least make sure that HR sees my application. I know this might not work, but I have to at least try. I threw this away, and I guess that saying's right: you don't really know what you've got until it's gone, and I miss Duke Capital. It was my first choice before Harrison Duke, and it's still my first choice.

With the job applied for, I'm still feeling jittery. Harrison's at work all day, and unpacking my meager possessions took less than an hour, so that's done. I check the time and see that it's almost eight a.m. Before I left New York, this is when I would've been finishing up my morning hip-hop class. If I hurry, I could still make the nine a.m. class. And maybe dancing—poorly—is just what I need to shake off the nerves.

I take the subway to get there, snapping a picture so that Harrison can see that there's nothing dangerous about it. Just me and a bunch of people on their phones or reading their books, on their way to start the day. I send it along with a cheeky text message: **Told you it wasn't scary! Don't worry. I've got this. *winking emoji***

It feels good to be out and about, moving through the crowds. There's something comforting about them, and when I walk up to the old gym that houses my dance class, I'm grinning from ear to ear. I can hear the warm-up music already playing as I walk in, and even the smell of the rubber floor mats combined with sweat is comforting. This is a city that's alive, and I'm right here in the heart of it. In fact, I'm practically buzzing with excitement.

Oh wait. Nope. I'm actually buzzing because my phone's ringing.

Harrison's name flashes across the screen, so I slide to answer it.

"Hey," I say. "I'm about to start a class. What's up?"

"Why were you on the subway? I thought we agreed you'd take a car."

"We never agreed," I reply. "Besides I didn't have time. Spontaneous decision. You know, like your spontaneous decision to take a jet to Kansas and seduce me."

I can hear the frustrated growl on the other end, and I giggle.

"This is serious," he says. "Where are you?"

"In my old neighborhood at the gym," I say. "I've got some dance classes that I already paid for, so I wanted to use them."

"That doesn't matter," he says. "Why can't you just go to a dance class in my neighborhood?"

"Because fancy spin classes aren't my thing," I say. "And anyway, I like this class. Which, speaking of, it's about to start, so I gotta go."

"Emery—"

"Harrison, relax," I nearly groan the reply. "It's daytime. I'm totally safe, and I'll see you tonight. But I gotta go now. Don't worry. I'll show off my moves for you later."

I'm fairly certain I can hear the eye-roll in his tone, but he acquiesces, and I shut off the phone just in time. They've just started doing hip thrusts when I run in and take my place at the back.

"Sorry I'm late!" I call to the instructor, a woman named Diana with the body of a nineties super model. I wish my abs looked like hers. I'm pretty sure she could crush cans with that six-pack.

"Get warm!" Diana shouts at me. "Big movements!"

I follow along, taken up immediately in the movement. I look like a complete idiot, but I don't care. It feels good to be moving freely. I'm throwing my arm to the left—a little more than I need to, honestly—when I smack right into a hard bicep.

"Oh snap!" I say. "Sorry."

I turn to said bicep and find that it's attached to a tall, handsome man. His blonde hair's cut close to his scalp, and his blue eyes shine when he smiles at me. He's executing the moves effortlessly, and I'm more than a little jealous of the way he moves easily through Diana's combinations.

"Snap?" he laughs, but it's friendly, not judgmental. "No apology needed," he adds with a grin. "I appreciate a girl who can dance with abandon."

I laugh. "Thank you, but I think lunacy is a better description of my moves."

He winks, giving me strong Channing Tatum vibes. "Well, whatever it is, it's pretty hot."

I know that it's not just the exercise that's heating me up. I blush, then turn back to focusing on the routine. I follow Diana and move through her next steps, lots of popping moves, and a few where I drop to the ground and move my hips as I come up. And even though I don't look, I have a feeling that hip-hop Channing over there is watching me.

In another life, he'd be totally my type. He's cool and charming and cute. But in this life? In this life, I'm all Harrison, all the time. I meant what I said to him. I'd never cheat. Besides all my thoughts are taken up by Harrison and his kisses and his *everything*.

Still, it's flattering to have a guy flirt with me, especially when I'm sweating my way through this workout. I make it to the end gasping for air but feeling exhilarated that I mastered the last few moves, and as I turn to grab my bag at the back, I find that Channing's lookalike is standing nearby.

"Hey," he says. "Great class, huh?"

I nod. "Totally."

"Dancing's always the best cardio," he says. "Well, second best."

He grins at that, and I don't miss the innuendo.

He shoulders a backpack. "So, you wanna go get a smoothie or something?"

I smile. "Sorry, I've got a boyfriend."

"Cool. Then I won't try to make out with you between sips. Come on, I know all the best combinations at the smoothie bar in this gym."

I bite my lip. I don't want to give this guy false hope, but I've been very clear, right?

"You can tell me about your boyfriend," he adds. "Come on, I hate to smoothie alone. My name's William by the way."

I smile at his easy nature. This guy is totally non-threatening. "Emery," I tell him. And because I never pass up a chance to talk about Harrison I start gushing. "He's the best. Very cool, mysterious, powerful...funny, too. And he really cares about things all the way around, not just the surface parts, you know? Everything."

William nods, walking us over to the smoothie bar as he orders something called The Muscle and another called The Lay-Up.

"Sounds like a good guy," he says. "And it sounds like he makes you happy. Are you allowed to have friends?"

"Of course," I reply with a roll of my eyes. But inside, I'm not entirely sure. No, I am. Of course I'm allowed to have friends. But I suspect that I know what Harrison's reaction to this guy would be, and it wouldn't be good. Because he's cute, and Harrison would be jealous. But it's not like I'm attracted to him. He's objectively attractive, yes, but that's not his fault and I already made it clear I'm not interested.

Harrison would probably enroll me in a senior citizen dance class if he saw this guy, I think, stifling a smile.

"Something funny?" William asks.

"No," I deflect, but I laugh cause it is kind of funny.

"Well then, here you go, friend." To sweeten the deal— literally—William hands me one of the smoothies he ordered. I take it and take a sip, tasting coconut water and raspberry. It's a good mix.

"Thanks." I grin. "See you next class maybe?"

He nods. "See you then."

I hit the showers, feeling buoyed by a successful class and the taste of the smoothie. By the time I'm dressed and on my way out the door I'm on the verge of going full Disney princess and whistling when, suddenly, I crash into a hulk of a man. He catches my wrist before I can drop the smoothie, thankfully.

Still, strange men shouldn't be grabbing me by the wrist, and I'm inches away from beating him with my gym tote when I realize I recognize the man. It's Bruce, one of Harrison's employees.

"Oh, Bruce," I say. "I wasn't expecting to see you. Is Harrison here?"

He shakes his head. "Nope. He asked me to come get you."

"Oh," I say, feeling slightly uncomfortable by the sudden appearance of Bruce, though I'm not totally sure why. "Well, I wasn't planning to go home yet."

"That's fine, Ms. Mills," he replies. "I'm assigned to you for the day. Wherever you want to go, I'll take you. I'm your driver."

Annoyance flares inside of me. I don't know where I want to go. I wanted to wander, enjoy the city, something that won't be easy to do with The Hulk needing to know exactly what my agenda is.

All I wanted was a life in New York, but I guess billionaire boyfriends come with driver-slash-bodyguards.

Sighing, I force myself to shake off my bad attitude. I'm being difficult for no reason. If Harrison is so worried, it's hardly a hardship for me to avoid the subway and use his driver. And I guess I can tell him to just drive around until I spy something interesting. If he's here, I might as well make the most of it. And besides, it's not him I'm annoyed at. It's Harrison, and I'll have to deal with that later.

I sigh. "All right, Bruce. I hope you like wandering."

CHAPTER TWENTY-FOUR

HARRISON

CATCHING up at the office hasn't been a nightmare, but it hasn't been a walk in the park, either. Sandy had to reschedule half a dozen meetings while I was gone, which means I'm booked back to back most of this week. Apparently, my opinions are necessary, as I'm known to be something of a control freak.

Which is fine by me. That's what it takes to put—and keep—Duke Capital at the top of the industry where it belongs. Besides which, when left to their own devices, my team isn't nearly aggressive enough.

Ramon tells me I'm being picky, but this is what it takes to be the CEO.

"We found four new leads," Ramon told me this afternoon with a laugh. "How many do you want, Harrison?"

"Double that," I told him, and he sighed. "More choices lead to stronger finds."

"You're right," he says. "We'll find more. But can I just tell you that it's good to see you happy?"

I know Ramon doesn't know exactly what happened in Kansas, but he spent the entire day giving me knowing looks and making comments like that. I haven't told anyone about

Emery being back, but somehow, he knows. And I'm not going to give him the satisfaction of asking how.

The rest of the day passes in a blur of work, but I don't mind. Work feeds into my adrenaline, and it distracts me from the idea of Emery and that damn subway.

Why can't she just wait for me to show her the city from the privacy of a luxury car? Or, better yet, I'll take her for a helicopter tour. I'll take her to every museum, every club, every sight that she wants to see. Private tours even. We could have any attraction she wants to see all to ourselves.

"Sir?"

The question's from the executive that's pitching me, and I realize I've been lost in thought. I wave at her to continue, and she gestures back to her presentation.

I'll focus on Emery later when I'm home. For now, I know she's safe with Bruce escorting her wherever. Which I'm sure doesn't thrill her, but if I can't be with her it's the next best thing.

————

WHEN I GET HOME, Emery isn't there. The space is clean and empty, per usual. For a moment, I think that maybe Kansas was just a fever dream, and that she never came back. But then I go to my bedroom and see her suitcase still in the closet, her clothes neatly hanging beside my own. I see her skincare and makeup on the bathroom counter.

So she's here, just not at home.

I get out my phone, ready to text her or Bruce. It's a little past seven, and I'd wanted to take her to dinner. I'm not sure if I'm a needy prick or if I'm actually seeing less of her now that she lives with me.

I shake my head, laughing at myself. Definitely being a needy prick.

Suddenly, footsteps outside the door, and then the key's turning. And there she is.

She's in jeans and a low-cut top, her hair thrown into a ponytail. She looks almost winded, slightly breathless. She drops her purse on the table near the door, and then her eyes sweep across the room.

Until they find me.

God, just the thought of her last night, those moans she made, the way she bit her lip and arched her back…my cock's twitching, my whole body aching for her. She's been gone too long.

Her eyes narrow at me, and at first, I think she's thinking the same thing. That it's lust. Then, she puts her hands on her hips and glares.

"You stuck a bodyguard on me?"

I start. "Technically, he's your driver."

She can't possibly be mad about this. Every other woman in New York—hell, the world—would kill to have someone at their beck and call, ready to take them wherever they want to go. Carry packages, find a parking space, hold umbrellas. Is she kidding me? And clearly, she made use of Bruce. She was out, doing God knows what all around town. I think of the gym he picked her up at this morning. A decrepit old building with crumbling steps and a cheap sign over the door. I should have it investigated for health code violations.

"Harrison," she snaps, drawing me back into the conversation. "I didn't ask for a bodyguard."

"You didn't have to," I say, grinning. "I was happy to do it."

Yeah, yeah. I get that she's annoyed, but what doesn't she understand? I'll give her anything she needs. Protection. Money. Whatever she wants.

"But I didn't ask for that," she repeats. "I told you that I liked the subway, and you just went and did this anyway."

"I wanted you to be safe," I object to her implication that

I'm overstepping. It's just security, it's not like I'm asking her to stay home.

"A week ago, I was by myself in another state," she says. "Alone. By myself. I'm an adult."

I don't want to point out that by herself she means living with her mother, in a town with a population of...I don't know. Twelve people? Fine, five hundred? A thousand? Jesus, the population of Park Ave alone is higher than that. There's a million and a half people in Manhattan and I trust about a dozen of them. Emery's so young, so inexperienced. She hasn't seen what this city's capable of. Good, yes. Great. Wonderful. But also, dangerous. And I'll be damned if I let anything bad happen to her.

"Bruce is just a driver," I tell her. "You're free to come and go as you please. Go wherever you want. This way, you have someone to get you anywhere you want to go safely and efficiently."

"You mean someone to watch me," she says.

God, she's hot when she's pissed. Her face is flushed, and she bites her lip as she waits for my response. I cross to her, leaving us only feet apart.

"I was just taking care of you," I say. "You had a need, and I fulfilled it."

The words are heavy with suggestion, and her tongue flicks across her lips before disappearing in her mouth. It leaves her lips glossy and slick, and the desire to draw her mouth to mine is overwhelming.

"You can't just decide for me, though," she says, tipping her chin up to look directly into my eyes as I move closer yet. "We have to *communicate*."

"Well then," I say, voice a low growl as I run a finger along her jaw. "Let me communicate my desire to keep you safe."

I kiss her, deep and needy. I need to show her how much she means to me. I need her to understand that her being here means everything, and I can't allow anything to jeopardize that.

Lifting my head, I tuck a hair behind her ear and look at her, her wide eyes glinting in the light. She smiles and presses a kiss to my jaw.

"I need you to trust me," she says. "Because I'd never do anything to ruin this."

I squeeze her against me, even as thoughts of what happened before threaten to infiltrate this moment. Thoughts about the agreement between her and Blythe. Hell, even Blythe herself. The way she took my trust and tossed it under a metaphorical speeding cab.

But Emery's right. She deserves to be trusted. She's not Blythe. She's perfect, and she's here, with me, in my home.

"I could be persuaded," I say, reaching down to caress her backside. "With a thought-provoking discussion, of course. If you were up to the task."

She bites her lip in response and moves in to kiss me again, and I can tell by the feel of her tongue against mine that it's going to be a good, long night.

CHAPTER TWENTY-FIVE

EMERY

WHEN I WAKE UP, Harrison's already left for work. He must've kissed me before he left, but after last night's activities, I'm not surprised that I could barely wake up. I smile at the memories, of Harrison inside of me, of his mouth on me, of this joy of waking up in his bed.

Also, who knew sex was this much fun? Not me, or I'd never have held out as long as I did. I think I'm developing a sex addition—to Harrison.

God, that man. As frustrated as I was when I got back last night, one look at him, and my resolve faltered. I know he's trying to protect me. I just wish he realized that I don't need to be protected.

A memory hits me. Blythe told me he was controlling. And, well, ten seconds with Harrison, and anyone would know that he's controlling. That he wants his hand in everything and wants to see every last detail addressed and accounted for. It's just frustrating to *be* a detail.

Ugh. I don't want Blythe to be right about anything, but I guess she was right about the controlling part. Still, I don't want to think about it.

I turn over in the bed, enjoying the warm sheets and the

giant bed. Every bed I've had in my life until now has been a twin. In Kansas, at school, my first New York apartment. Beds so small I could move a few inches and fall right off. But here? In Harrison's bed? I can fan out my arms and legs like a starfish and not even come close to falling out.

I'm still smiling and starfish-ing when my phone buzzes. I turn it over and find a text from Harrison that he sent earlier.

Harrison: **You were sleeping like the dead this morning. Tried to wake you, but you weren't having it. See you tonight.**

I smile at the phone like a schoolgirl. Ugh. Good thing no one can see me because it's ridiculous. But I don't care. I have a boyfriend. An amazing, incredible, thoughtful boyfriend. Who, yes, is a little controlling. But he's learning. I think.

I check for the message that just made my phone buzz in the first place, and it's a text from Ramon. My heart races and I sit up immediately.

Ramon: **There's an open position in marketing that's interviewing today. I can get you on the interview schedule if you can be here by ten. Let me know.**

It takes everything in me not to type "Hell yes I'll be there!" because I don't think that's very professional. But I do quickly respond that, yes, I'll be there, and then I nearly trip as I run from the bed to the shower.

I have an interview. An *interview*. And I got it all on my own, no interfering—but unfailingly handsome—boyfriend required.

I squeal. I race about getting ready for the interview, knowing that I can ace this. I can land it.

And I can start building my own dream right from scratch.

———

I MAKE it to Duke Capital ten minutes early in my favorite business appropriate dress. It makes me feel like a grown-up professional and it skims my curves in a way that still feels feminine. I added a pearl necklace that was a gift from my mom when I graduated college and I finger it mindlessly as I wait in the reception before my interview.

Bruce was waiting for me in the lobby of Harrison's apartment building this morning, and I have to admit I was grateful that he was there. I could've made my own way to Duke Capital, absolutely, but getting a ride gave me time to process and getting dropped off at the front door did not suck. Not even a little. And Bruce is kinda fun, Mr. Hulk and all. He'd laughed when I told him I needed to make it there for a ten a.m. interview.

"What's so funny?" I'd asked him.

"Why are you interviewing when you're dating the boss? Couldn't you just ask Harrison for whatever job you wanted?" Bruce had replied, catching my eye in the rearview mirror.

"Could and should are two very different things," I said. "I know I'm qualified for this job. And I don't want to get anything in life based on someone else's accomplishments."

He'd shrugged, nodding his head. "Good for you, Ms. Mills."

"Bruce," I'd corrected. "What did I tell you?"

"You know I can't call you Emery," he'd said back. "Against my official code."

I'd rolled my eyes. It felt so formal, having him call me Ms. Mills. I'd never had someone reporting to me in my entire life, not a housekeeper or a gardener or anything like that. We did everything ourselves, and it was odd to have someone that was basically my employee. But if I had to have a driver, at least it was Bruce, and he was cool.

He's wrong, though, about asking Harrison for a job. Duke Capital is a massive company, and I'm determined to fit into it with nothing but my own gumption and qualifications. They might be limited, my qualifications, but they're good. And my potential is sky high, if I say so myself.

Besides, Ramon sent me more about the job. It's not an internship. It's a real, entry-level job where I'd have a clear path to working my way up the corporate ladder. I'd be able to actually make decisions, albeit not a lot of them, but still. I'd have an actual role here. Something to be proud of. Something that's mine.

"Ms. Mills?"

A woman with close cropped red hair appears with a smile. She's probably in her late forties, with a power suit and a kind smile. I decide she'll make the perfect boss.

And even though I've been wrong about that before, I push the thought aside.

"Come in," she says.

She waves me into a conference room and has me take a seat across from her.

"I'm Bethany," she says, introducing herself. "I appreciate you coming in on such short notice."

"Absolutely," I say. "I appreciate the opportunity."

I smile, and she smiles back.

"Well then…" She nods, looking over what I assume is my resume as she speaks, her eyes flickering back and forth from me to the paper. "Ramon tells me you worked here before? As an intern?"

I nod. "I did. But I'm eager to move into something more permanent. I loved interning here and I'm confident I'd be a great fit in marketing."

"What were some of your responsibilities?"

The words "Coffee Girl" flit across my mind. But I know I did way more than that, and I tell her. I tell her about all of my experience working with Ramon on Pink, on how I helped Harrison at the conference—though I leave out the part about us sleeping together. If Bethany knows about our relationship, she doesn't say anything, which I appreciate.

"And I'm a quick learner," I tell her. "Anything I don't already know, I'll figure it out. Google's my best friend, basically."

She laughs. "I love a girl who does her own research. So why don't you—"

Suddenly, there's a knock at the conference door. I turn, and my heart drops and leaps at the same time.

It's Harrison.

"Bethany," he says, his voice cool. "Pardon the interruption."

She nods. "It's okay, Mr. Duke. Did you need the conference room?"

He shakes his head. "I actually wanted to step in on this interview. If you don't mind." He inclines his head a fraction towards the door.

Bethany nods, clearly getting the message that step in meant take over. She grabs her notes and stands. "Of course."

If she thinks it's odd that the CEO is taking over the interview, she doesn't say anything. Instead, she reaches out and shakes my hand, smiling the entire time.

"It was a pleasure to meet you, Ms. Mills," she says.

Then, her voice drops a bit as she says, "Good luck."

Good luck?

Did I...did I fuck up by not telling Harrison that I was interviewing?

Oh shit. Does he think I'm going behind his back?

I turn to look at him as he takes the seat that Bethany was just in. He's running his tie between his fingers as he rocks in the chair a bit, eyeing me. Then with a grin, he begins writing neatly across a notepad he brought in with him. I strain to read the words, but he looks up, catching me in the act.

"I'm not going to go easy on you, you know," he says. "This is my company, and I take it very seriously."

I straighten my back. I can work with that. I don't want special treatment, anyway.

"I understand, Mr. Duke."

His lips twitch.

"Perfect," he says. "Then let's begin."

CHAPTER TWENTY-SIX

HARRISON

GOD, she was so adorable applying for a job through HR. As if she actually needed anyone's approval but mine. As if I'd deny her anything she asked for.

In a way, I appreciate it. I appreciate that Emery went about this the hard way. She didn't ask for a handout. She did her best to apply without involving me, for a position that was already open and needed to be filled. She wanted to work for it and prove her mettle.

Ramon was the one who brought it to my attention. She'd asked him if he could provide a recommendation. Which answered how the sneaky bastard knew Emery was back in the first place. I don't know whether to be impressed with the fact that he kept that to himself in order to gloat or to roll my eyes at the way he attempted to playfully goad me when he told me that Emery was applying for an entry-level job.

As if she didn't know that she was leagues better than that job.

I told Ramon to find a job in marketing for her. I'd seen firsthand—and Ramon had too—that she had a natural skill for it. In fact, I'd love to put her back on the Pink project with

Ramon. It's where she'll sing. But let her interview for this position with Bethany first. Let's see what she says.

I didn't tell Bethany about Emery. I wanted it to be clean, a true evaluation of Emery's abilities. One look at Bethany's face as she was leaving told me all I needed to know, and that was that Emery had knocked it out of the fucking park.

Not that she's out of the woods yet. I have my own questions for her, and I wasn't lying about not taking it easy on her. If she wants to earn this job, then she'll fucking earn it.

"So," I say. "Tell me about your goals."

She tucks a loose strand of hair from behind her ear before moving her hands out of sight under the table. I can imagine that she's wringing them in her lap from nervousness, but she's hiding it well on the surface at least. The lipstick she painted on this morning is bright red, and my cock twitches at the thought of that color smeared after taking me in her mouth.

"I'm a hard worker," she says. "Whatever I do, I give my all. If something's wrong, I'll figure out a way to fix it."

"Why would there be something wrong?" I ask, leaning back as I add to my notes. "Are you suggesting you'd be careless on a project in the first place?"

That flusters her. "Of course not. I just know that sometimes, things come up."

"Ms. Mills," I say. "This is a billion dollar company. Are you saying you'd make a mistake?"

"I'd do my best not to," she says. "But if I did, I'd own up to it. And I'd fix it."

"Hmm," I murmur in response. I relish that she doesn't fall apart at this line of questioning. I've seen men well into their fifties fumble that question.

"Let's move on to your strengths," I say. "Tell me about those."

I could give a list of her strengths. Bedroom strengths, sure, but more than that, her attention to detail, her commitment, her ability to charm every coworker and client. The way she's not afraid to speak her mind.

"I've learned that there aren't no-win situations," she says. "Before, I thought that some situations were just doomed to not turn out the way I wanted them to. But I've learned that fighting for something is important, and I'm a fighter. I won't give up on something I believe in."

I know she's talking marketing, but I can't help but think she's also talking about us. She could've turned me away when I showed up in Kansas. Hell, she could've taken Blythe's money and written it all off as a loss. But she didn't. She kept going for me. For us.

"What else?" I say, standing up to pace behind the table. I walk slowly across the room to stand behind her, waiting for her to respond.

This catches her off guard. She gave a pitch perfect response, and she knows it. I watch from behind as she bites her lip, thinking about what to say.

"Um, I'm pretty—"

"You are," I agree, no longer able to keep up with the pretense that she's just another interview.

"Harrison," Emery chides, dragging my name out while tilting her head to the side in slight exasperation. "I'm trying to be serious here."

I smirk. Part of me—the part thinking only with my cock —wants to fuck her right now on this table. She looks incredible, her lips pouting as she looks back at me with challenge in her eyes. But as much as I want her in this moment, I also know that this is a big deal for her. She wouldn't have applied for this behind my back if she didn't want to get this on her own. I respect her drive enough to table my own lust and focus on her.

I step back and pace again around the table, then come to stand at the end as I think on my next question.

"What changes would you make here at Duke Capital, if you could?"

This question is a bigger trap than people think it is. A cocky asshole might come here and start a laundry list of grievances that he's got against the company. This tells me right away that he's going to be a problem, not because I have a problem with critique, but because he's clearly not a fan of how I run my business. He'd also be likely to place blame on others and not take responsibility.

The other wrong answer to this question is to say there are no changes to be made. Every organization has room for growth, and having outside eyes makes a business stronger. But the response I'm looking for here needs to show an understanding of the company's values while still finding something to improve on.

Emery worries her lip as she thinks. She's smart to not just launch into an answer. She's really considering it.

She opens her mouth to answer, and then, suddenly, there's a knock on the conference room door before it flies open without waiting on a response.

There, standing in the door, is Blythe. She doesn't look surprised to see us. In fact, she looks like a cat that's caught a mouse, and her lips curl up with a devilish grin.

"Oops," she says. "I thought Bethany had this room. I'm sorry for, uh, interrupting your little *visit*."

I don't miss the insinuation, and neither does Emery. Her cheeks burn as she looks at the table, her eyes narrowed.

It's such a bullshit lie, too. She must've seen Emery and Bethany go in, or maybe she saw it on the schedule. And I'm sure she saw me go in after. She likely hoped to catch us in a compromising position, and I'm glad there's an entire conference room table between Emery and myself. Blythe's a damn snake, but at least she didn't get what she wanted.

Not that it fucking matters. This is my company. I'll run it how I see fit and my relationship with Emery has nothing to do with Emery's potential. I'm about to say something, but Emery speaks before I have a chance to.

"It's a great question, Mr. Duke," she says in a cheery voice, eyes cutting from Blythe and back to me as she smiles. "In terms of changes I'd want to make, I think I'd adjust some of the personnel. I'd want to make sure that everyone working at Duke Capital understands the potential of this organization and that they share in its vision. Having forward thinking people in *every* role is essential to both an ethical and successful company."

She doesn't look back at Blythe, but Blythe's face falls as if she's been slapped. She glares at me.

"I'd also invest in worthwhile charities," Emery continues. "Ensure proper vetting is done into each of them. In fact, I'd love to talk about a plan to pair specific projects with specific charities."

Now, she looks over her shoulder at Blythe. "But given the sensitivity and intricacy of that plan, I'll hold off on that for now."

There's nothing rude about her tone. Her smile hasn't moved in inch. But the middle finger to Blythe is clear, and I can see my ex-wife practically vibrating with rage.

"Thank you, Ms. Mills," I say. "I think you're right. Moving on—Blythe, did you need something?"

I ask the question with as little emotion in my tone as I can manage, trying not to smile too broadly at the roundhouse kick of a response that Emery just gave.

"I thought Bethany might want some input about Emery from her former boss," Blythe says, still glowering at Emery. "So—"

"Then you should go find her," I deadpan. "While I wrap this up."

"I—"

"Blythe," I say, voice ice cold with warning. "Close the door behind you."

Blythe looks from me to Emery in disbelief. Emery tucks a loose hair behind her ear and then sits forward in her seat, innocently blinking at me.

Behind her, Blythe seems to consider saying something else, but in the end, she just turns around and slams the door shut.

After she leaves, Emery gives me a full grin and even a relieved laugh.

"That was awesome," she says.

And I can't think of a better word to describe it. It *was* awesome.

Fuck. She's incredible. I can't get over the fact that she put Blythe in her place. Or that she thought she needed to apply for a position here, and that she was willing to take whatever crappy job was available, even with everything she went through before. Not that any job at Duke Capital is crappy, per se, but she's so far beyond what she applied for. She'd be far better suited for account management, especially given her answers to these interview questions.

I have something in mind, just for her, because I'll be damned if we stick her in a position she can't shine in.

CHAPTER TWENTY-SEVEN

EMERY

I'VE NEVER BEEN SO excited to fill out paperwork in my entire life.

Because…I got the job!

Okay, yes obviously I knew I was going to get it. And yes, I tried to get it without involving Harrison, but once he knew I'd applied I suppose it was a done deal. Imagine if I hadn't? We'd have been in for a whole lot of awkward dinners at home.

He didn't hire me on the spot though.

Instead he'd tried to play it off like it wasn't his call and he was going to leave it up to the hiring manager. I imagine he left absolutely nothing up to her, but at least I felt pretty confident that I'd charmed Bethany on my own merits. I'm hopeful that she liked me enough not to resent that she has to hire me.

Because I'm really, really excited about going back to work.

When HR had called with the offer I'd silently hopped up and down in excitement while verbally accepting the job. That evening Harrison ordered in some dessert from a local bakery, and we ate tiramisu in celebration of my victory. I feel like I've landed on top of the world, and absolutely nothing can change my mind.

"I can't believe you're so excited," Harrison says with a smile, adjusting his tie in the mirror as I try to decide between the different work outfits that I've laid out on the bed. "It's the same place you worked at before. You know that, right?"

"Yeah, but I was just an intern," I say. "And now, I have my own job. I get my own cubicle. I've already been envisioning it, the theme I'm going for."

Harrison snorts. "Your cubicle's going to have a theme?"

"Of course," I say, deadly serious. "I need to send a message that I'm both creative and professional. I'm thinking maybe mint with metallic gold for the color scheme, but that might be too much. I haven't decided."

"You have a theme and a color scheme?"

"They feed each other."

"Of course." Harrison nods supportively but his tone is lacking the appropriate enthusiasm if you ask me.

"Plus, now I get benefits and a 401k!" I bounce a little because this is a really exciting step in adulthood.

"I'll give you a benefit right now," Harrison teases as he passes behind me, patting me on my ass as he does.

"Stop, I cannot be late for my first day."

"You could, actually. I could write you a note."

I roll my eyes in his face to let him know I don't think he's funny and return to the important business of selecting my outfit.

I've picked out a pale blue suit and a pair of cream-colored heels. It's an outfit that one of Harrison's personal shoppers picked out for me, and it's something I never would've considered on my own. But the suit especially is so lush and looks fantastic on me. Especially my ass. But in like a cool, professional way.

I change into it, watching Harrison's eyes peek at me in the mirror's reflection. I give him a nice view of the pants sliding up over my curves and let him watch as my lacy white bra disappears under my button-down shirt and suit jacket.

"Don't worry," I tell him. "I'll let you undress me later."

"In my office?" he asks, a flirty smile on his lips.

"Absolutely not!" I shake my head, and I'm somewhat serious. "We can't make that a habit, you know. I'm a professional woman now."

"So I was only allowed to fuck you at work when you were an intern? Maybe this promotion was a mistake."

I roll my eyes. "It's not exactly a promotion. It's an entry-level marketing job. Like a lateral move."

"You moved from intern to something else. Sounds like a promotion to me."

"Whatever." I shrug, but I'm grinning. I know the shine will probably wear off soon, but for now it feels so good to be earning my own paycheck again. I don't care how small that paycheck is either. Even if it's a two dollar increase from my internship, it'll be worth it.

"I got something for you," Harrison says, waving me out to the kitchen. "Open it, and then we'll head to the office together."

My grin expands. No more sneaking into the office at different times. We're together and he doesn't care who knows it. And I don't care who knows it, either, since I *know* I'm capable and qualified and willing to prove myself to anyone who thinks otherwise.

But first, it sounds like Harrison got me a present, which has me nearly skipping to the kitchen in anticipation.

Big black box. Huge red bow. I gingerly undo the ribbon and find the world's most gorgeous bag hiding under the most perfectly folded tissue paper. The bag is navy with pebbled leather and golden hardware, and I literally gasp out loud at the sight of it.

It's a grown-up bag. A modern day feminine briefcase, one

I can slip a laptop inside of along with whatever personal items I want to bring to and from work. It's got a fancy designer label on it and I suspect it cost more than I make in a month.

"I hope you like it," Harrison says with all the casualness of someone who just gifted a cup of coffee. "But I've got other options coming tomorrow. This is just so you had something for today. If you like it, we'll get it monogrammed."

My head whips to him. "What?"

"Well, I wanted to make sure you had something for your first day," he says. "But I also wanted to give you choices in case you hated it."

"I don't hate it, I love it," I say, clutching the bag to my chest. It's perfect and it makes my heart flutter that he went through the trouble of getting it for me and making sure it was here for my first day.

"You're spoiling me, you know that?" I say, pulling him into a kiss. "I love it. Thank you."

He smiles back, and I can tell that he's pleased.

"Well, let's make sure you're not late for your first day," he says. "Or the boss might just have to come down on you hard."

I laugh, and we head downstairs. It's Leo this time, and as much as I like Bruce, it gives me comfort to see Leo. He nods to me as Harrison and I enter the car.

"Wonderful to see you, Ms. Mills."

Like Bruce, I'm pretty sure he'll never call me by my first name. But that's okay. I catch up with him and show off my fancy new briefcase. He gives lots of compliments on it and my suit, and I feel like I'm walking on clouds by the time we get to Duke Capital.

My first day. It's more exciting than a first day of school. I can't wait.

"I'm going to stop and get a coffee before I head up," I tell Harrison. "See you at lunch?"

"I'll come down to get you," he says.

"Oh no," I object. "You can't be lurking around my cube during work hours, Mr. Duke. People will think I have preferential treatment."

He smirks, the smile tugging at his lips in a way that does it for me every time. "You do, though."

I sigh, exasperated. "But I don't need to advertise it on the first day."

"Fine," Harrison teases. "You can meet Leo outside. I'll be waiting in the car like your dirty little secret."

"Perfect!" I tease back and add a little wink. Then I clip my way over to the Starbucks in the lobby. I don't really need coffee since I'm already so hyped, but it gives me a second to start my day on my own terms. As much as I love arriving to work with Harrison, I'm doing my very best to make it clear that I and I alone will be responsible for my trials and tribulations here at Duke Capital.

After grabbing my coffee, I head up to the HR office. I smile at the receptionist.

"Hi there," I say. "Emery Mills, here for my first day."

The girl snorts. "Isn't it your second first day?"

My smile falters, but I toss my hair back. "My first day not as an intern."

She nods, fishing out some paperwork that she passes over to me.

"Well, since you know the drill, this should go quickly," she says. "You'll see the job title and description are there, along with the salary—"

"Holy shit!"

My eyes boggle when I see the number. It's a six figure number. And it's nearly triple what I was making as an intern.

"I think you gave me the wrong paperwork," I say, scanning through the job quickly. It says "Account Manager, Marketing" at the top. I interviewed for a marketing associate position and this isn't anything like what Bethany and I talked about.

The girl rolls her eyes. Does Harrison know he has this much sass in HR? Never mind. No need to involve him.

The girl says, "Your name's on the document, isn't it?"

And I look. It is. But what the hell? This isn't the entry-level job I applied for. This is like, five huge leaps forward. And as I'm reading, I see words like "manage accounts," which… that's not Bethany's department. That's Ramon's and Harrison's.

Did Harrison change this? Did he bait and switch me…on a freaking job?

My hand shakes as I stare at the paper. I'm so furious that I'm literally seeing red. The HR girl's watching me.

"Are you okay?" she asks. "You look, uh, weird."

All I can do is focus on the job description. The details.

Job will require exceptional attention to detail and a take-charge attitude. Job candidates must be problem solvers and independent thinkers.

All the requirements are carefully written to fit me. It's all of my strengths rolled into one job. Hell, it's all of the things I loved doing before I left for Kansas. It's, fuck it, it's *perfect* for me. This is the kind of job I'd kill for, one that I envisioned as a dream job. But I wasn't applying for my dream job.

I was applying for an entry-level job. A start.

I want to barge into Harrison's office right now and ask him what the hell he thinks he's doing. But then I start to wonder. Did Harrison know this job would be perfect for me? Is this about him trying to control my life or give me something I haven't earned? Or is this him giving me a great opportunity at something I can absolutely handle?

Is this his way of showing he cares about me? About my career potential and not just as his girlfriend?

"I'm fine," I tell the HR girl. "I'll just take a seat and sign everything."

She nods, and I sit, staring at the words, at the salary, at everything. Harrison might've helped redirect my application in a way, but I'm made for this job. And I fully intend to prove that I deserve it.

Though I'm still not sure if Harrison is getting a thank you at lunch or a piece of my mind.

CHAPTER TWENTY-EIGHT

HARRISON

SHE'S LATE FOR LUNCH.

I'm waiting in the car for her, turning my wrist over again and again to check the time on my Rolex. She should be here by now, but she's not.

Did something go wrong?

It strikes me that maybe I shouldn't have meddled. Or at least, maybe I should've given her a heads-up about giving her a marketing executive job with Ramon as her supervisor.

But she needs to stop shortchanging herself. That entry-level job was beneath her, and very nearly an insult, not just to her but to my company. I've never been the kind of CEO who believes in playing explicitly by the rules. Find a good lead? Follow it. Figure out a quicker way to solve a problem? If it's legal, then do it. And if you find good talent, then for fuck's sake, use the talent.

Emery's a talent. She's got a raw gift for this business and the hunger to chase it. Putting her anywhere else would just be a fucking waste.

Besides. It's my company. My call.

Maybe she's worried about what people will say. That she slept her way into this job? But that would be bullshit, and I'd be the first one to shut that talk down. Bethany was sorely disappointed I told her she'd have to find another candidate for the position Emery was interviewing for. But even Bethany understood that Emery would've outgrown that job in months, probably weeks. Better to put her somewhere where she can put her quick learning skills to good use.

And fuck, do I know that she's a quick learner.

Because she's got an insatiable appetite for both business and sex. Which is just fine by me. Hell if I don't know what a lucky bastard that makes me. God, if I could spend the rest of my life coaxing those perfect little gasps and groans out of her it would be time well spent.

But will I get the chance? Or is she so furious with me for interfering with her job that she's quit? Did she leave this morning? I should call HR. I've just gotten my phone out to dial when Leo clears his throat.

"I believe that's Ms. Mills now, sir," he says, pointing in the direction of the building.

There she is in that suit. It's hugging her curves in all of the right places, and her hips swing with each step of her heels. I can't read her expression as she walks up to the car.

"Leo, we might need some privacy," I mutter, resigned to whatever's coming. "Can you just head in the direction of the restaurant?"

"Of course, sir," he says, rolling up the partition before Emery steps into the car.

"Hello," I say cautiously as she slides in next to me.

She tosses back her hair, looking at me in what I swear is a mischievous way. As she does, Leo pulls out of the spot, the car merging into New York traffic.

"Well hello to you too," she drawls. "Was there something you forgot to tell me?"

Shit. She is mad. She doesn't look mad, but there's something simmering there beneath the surface. An expression that I still can't quite read, but I'm not quite stupid enough to miss it.

"I made a decision," I say. "As CEO of the company, it's my call to make."

"Oh?" Emery says, lifting an eyebrow. "This was purely a tycoon power move?"

"Absolutely," I reply, trying not to smile at her sassy tycoon comment. "I didn't get to where I am without the ability to recognize talent and assign it where it would most benefit Duke Capital."

She purses her lips. "Really? That's the story you're going with?"

"Look," I interject. "If you're mad, then—"

She holds up a finger and scoots closer to me.

"No," she says, shaking her head back and forth. "I want you to tell me exactly why you did this. You tell me why, and then I'll tell you what I'm feeling."

Fuck, she looks hot. I can just imagine her tongue licking that pointed finger up and down the way I know she can lick my cock. And the way her eyes are slightly hooded with what I can only assume is anger... I shouldn't be turned on, but my dick's already hardening in my pants.

"I thought you could do better," I tell her. "I care about your future, and that entry-level job was beneath you. Your internship alone would have qualified you for a better position than what you applied for and I wanted to give you the chance to do something worthwhile. To show everyone how qualified you are. Something as important and deserving as you are."

She watches me, and I breathe in deeply. I can smell her perfume, and it's heady and intoxicating this close in the car. I don't know if what I said is what she wants to hear, but it's the truth, dammit.

She wets her lips with her tongue. "You think I'm good

enough to go from being an intern to being an account manager?"

I can't tell if it's sarcasm dripping from her words or something else. I'm so distracted by the wet of her lips. All I can think about is whether or not her pussy is that same kind of wet, slick and waiting for me to fill her up.

"I think," I say very slowly. "That you can do anything you please."

It doesn't happen immediately. For a moment, nothing shows on her expression. Then, her lips curve into a smile and her doe eyes flutter.

"That's the right answer," she says.

Within seconds, she's straddled me. I don't waste any time and grab the full curve of her ass as I meet her lips in a crushing kiss. She grinds against me, feeling the heavy throb of my cock through both of our pants. I tear at the buttons of her blouse until her tits are freed, and then I palm both of them in my hands. She's kissing me back as she tugs off the suit jacket and then the button-down and then her bra, letting her tits bounce in front of my face. I pull a dusky peak into my mouth and suck hard, and she groans, biting down on her lip to smother the sound.

Thank fucking God for tinted windows. Still, the thrill of how she didn't give a damn, how her want overpowered everything else, is enough to make me nearly explode right now. I suck hard on her nipples as she continues to move against my cock, and I need her, need that tight little pussy around my cock right now.

I push down on her pants, and she stands a bit, bumping her head against the roof of the car. She shimmies out of her pants as I pull down her panties, and then she's completely naked for me. Completely naked and absolutely perfect, flushed pink on her cheeks and her breasts. I bet that swollen little pussy is flushed and soaking wet for me, too.

I'll need to check, of course. I rim a fingertip around her

opening, and she moans in response against the seat next to my face. I turn my head and kiss her as I thrust first one finger then two inside of her, loving how her pussy clamps around my fingers, begging for more.

Fuck, I wish I could taste her, but more than anything, I need to feel those soft thighs spread open across my lap. Need her to ride me the way she was just grinding against me.

———

"HANG ON," I say, using my free hand to dig my wallet out of my back pocket so I can grab a condom. I rip the black and gold wrapper quickly, and Emery seizes the condom from me, clearly not wanting my other hand to stop its thrusts inside of her. Still kissing me, our tongues clashing together, she rolls it on swiftly, and the feel of her hand pushing that condom down sends every last drop of blood down into my cock. I give one last teasing circle to her clit and pull my fingers out of her, and immediately, she sits down on me, driving my cock up inside of her in a single movement.

It's impossible not to let out a grunt of pleasure at the swiftness of the sensation, at the way her pussy swallows me completely. Emery returns to grinding against me, and I know she's rocking herself to get friction against her clit. She's buried her face in my neck as she moans and gasps, and I bite my lip to keep from coming like a bomb. I won't, not until she's used me to bring herself to orgasm.

It doesn't take long, and when she comes, there's no holding back the rush of my name on her lips. I come at the same time, driven almost insane at the feel of her tits bouncing against me, at the feel of her luscious ass cupped in my hands as I grip and squeeze.

When we're done, she's panting next to me, and I help her

back into her clothes. She's still catching her breath when she digs out her phone.

"Fuck," she says, and I lean over to look at the clock showing that we're both due back at the office very, very soon.

"It looks like we won't have time for lunch," she says.

She looks worried, and then she catches my smirking expression. Her lips curl into a grin, and then she kisses me again.

"I'd say it was worth it," she says. "And I do mean *all* of it. Though, in the future, I'd say it'd be nice to have a heads-up about any behind-the-scenes interventions."

"Then perhaps you shouldn't do such a thorough job of rewarding me," I say. "I might get the wrong idea."

She swats at me, but her grin's wide. "It wouldn't kill you to stock this car with granola bars or something. If you're going to insist on using my lunch hour to have your way with me."

"Tsk," I object, while fixing my tie. "You jumped me."

"Fine," her head drops against the seat, a tiny smile playing at her lips. "I'll buy the granola bars, you cheap bastard."

"I meant every word you know," I tell her, smiling in return. "You can do anything. I have every confidence in you."

She kisses me again, and the taste of her is so incredible, so addicting, that I have a feeling that there are a lot of long lunches in my future.

"That's why you get me so excitable," she says, blinking those long eyelashes at me. "Because you believe in me, and because you listened to me."

"And because you can't resist me," I remind her.

She rolls her eyes but doesn't argue.

How can she after how we just used our lunch hour?

CHAPTER TWENTY-NINE

EMERY

AFTER MY FIRST week on the job, Harrison insists we celebrate in some way. I expect him to suggest a quiet but expensive meal for the two of us, but instead, he tells me he was thinking of a dinner party where I could invite some folks from work along with my friends.

"My old roommates, you mean?" I asked, a little dubious considering their last interaction.

He laughed. "Yes. They're important to you, so they're important to me. Besides, your friends should see how happy you are."

I'd blushed, and then I'd kissed him, and then I'd—enthusiastically—agreed to the idea. After all, it *would* be great to celebrate my new job. I'd been kicking ass at work, and it wasn't just me who was saying so. Ramon's noticed and told me that he'd never seen someone take to a job the way I have. I'd made a point to learn everything there is to know about Duke's current profile, beyond just my own accounts. I'd also charmed all of our clients, and Monica over at Pink was especially thrilled to hear I'd been assigned to lead her account.

So yes, I think I deserve a little celebration. And a dinner party sounds fancy as hell.

Growing up, my mom never threw "dinner parties," or at least, she never called them that. Mom would just invite people over and make a ton of food, and people would eat sitting in whatever chair they could find. Sometimes it was the sofa, sometimes it was on patio furniture, but the most important thing was that there was good food on paper plates so that she didn't have to "spend half her life doing the damn dishes."

A New York dinner party is definitely not the same thing.

Harrison hires his usual chef, plus an army of caterers and staff to decorate and serve the entire event. It all seems preposterous to me since we're only inviting my roommates and a few people from work, basically Sandy and Ramon and a few other executives. But Harrison tells me that we're celebrating me, and if I'm the one being celebrated, he doesn't want me to have to lift a finger.

"What if I have to lift that finger to undo your belt?" I counter, teasing him while we're getting dressed for the party.

"After, you're allowed to do all the lifting you want," he says. "And maybe during any boring parts, you can run those talented little hands of yours up and down my cock."

I shiver. Just those words make me want to rip off the clothes that we just put on. He's in an incredible, fitted suit, and I'm in a slinky silver dress and heels. It feels weird to dress up to stay home, but we are entertaining. God, that sounds so cool.

So adult. So real life.

Harrison's phone buzzes, and he checks it and smiles.

"Your guests are arriving, Ms. Mills," he says with a wink.

"Well, we better go greet them, Mr. Duke."

I link my arm in his, and we head downstairs to the kitchen and living area, butterflies in my stomach even though it's just, really, hanging out with friends. Nothing major. Sure, people are meeting each other for the first time, but otherwise, nothing. No big deal.

"Enjoy yourself," Harrison whispers, the warmth of his breath tickling my ear. "You deserve it."

I smile and straighten my back, heading into the living room to welcome people.

Ramon shows up first, his beautiful wife and adorable kids in tow. As soon as the kids are in, the boy bolts for the leather couch and launches himself on it like he's an airplane.

"Uh, son, maybe don't jump on the furniture," Harrison says as he walks over to the child. "You might—"

But the kid takes off before Harrison can finish his sentence, racing a beeline for a display of whiskey glasses lined up near the bar.

"Don't touch that," Harrison says, following the kid. "No, not that either—"

Ramon smiles, watching Harrison. "Well, that ought to keep him busy."

I'm not sure who he's talking about, Harrison or the kid. But the kid clearly senses the thrill of the chase because he books down the hallway and out of sight. Harrison follows him, still trying to reason with the kid as he follows him around the corner.

"It's nice to have someone else chase him for a change," Ramon's wife says with a laugh, her dark brown eyes shimmering under black eyeliner. She extends her hand and smiles.

"I'm Anita," she says. "You must be Emery. It's a pleasure to meet you."

"You too," I say. "I'm really glad you could come. And who's this?"

I gesture to the shy girl hiding behind Ramon's pant leg. She's ridiculously cute with silky black hair tied into a braid. She twists the corner of her lilac dress in one hand and sucks her thumb with the other.

"This is Gabriela," Ramon says. "Gabby, why don't you say hi to Emery?"

I drop down to my knees and smile. "I really like your dress. Purple's one of my favorite colors."

That gets me a smile. She drops her dress and points at mine.

"I like yours," she says.

"She's obsessed with sparkles," Ramon says. "Loves glitter, too. Loves putting glitter everywhere in the house, actually."

I grin. "Gabby, do you want to come get some snacks with me?"

She lights up and nods, a girl after my own heart.

"Mind if I steal your kid?" I ask Ramon and Anita.

"Steal away!" Ramon says. "Between you and Harrison, we might be able to catch our breath for a moment."

I let Gabby take the lead. She puts her hand in mine and I follow her to the dessert table. Even though we haven't eaten anything yet, I help her sneak a mini-cupcake off the table and make her pinky swear not to tell. She grins and we fill up our plates with bread and cheese and fruit, munching and talking about the merits of Paw Patrol as we wind our way through the apartment. We've landed on her favorite—Skye— when her older brother zooms past us, a thoroughly out of breath Harrison trailing him.

"He doesn't stop," Ramon warns, walking up to us. Gabby squeals at the sight of her dad.

"Dad! I was telling Emery about Skye, and she said she'll watch with me!"

"Did she?" Ramon asks, smiling at me. "Well, she's pretty nice, isn't she? Why don't you go tell your mom about it?"

Gabby grins and bolts off to find her mom.

"Looks like chasing Cesar went well," Ramon says, smirking at Harrison. "You're out of breath, and he's not. Whew it's nice to have a night off," he adds with a grin.

Cesar is definitely not out of breath. He's run over to the

food trays and is loading up his own plate in the shape of a tower, much to the server's noticeable terror.

"Can't you kennel him?" Harrison asks, rolling his eyes.

"Ha! Good thing you're never having kids." Ramon laughs.

I laugh, too, waiting for Harrison to correct him. Only, he doesn't.

"I need a drink," he says instead. "God. This is why I only do things I know I'm good at."

Wait…no kids? I watch Harrison head over to the bar, blinking after him. I turn and find Ramon watching me.

"You're great with them, you know," he says. "Kids, I mean."

Is he reading my mind? And if he is, what does that mean?

"I like kids," I say, honestly. "I like their energy."

"You might not like it 24/7," Ramon says. "But then again…"

His eyes light on Anita. She's bouncing Gabby in her arms while Cesar zooms like an airplane around her legs. Her smile's radiant, and so are the kids'.

"They might just steal your heart," Ramon says.

I'm feeling some type of way about it when, suddenly, the door flings open and my old roommates appear. Their mouths open in shock as they look around, and I excuse myself from Ramon to greet them.

"You didn't tell us he lives in a penthouse," Sherri basically hisses.

"Girl, marry him," Dana says with a laugh. "Marry him now."

I smile back, but something in my heart tightens.

If he doesn't want kids, what else doesn't he want? Marriage? Forever? Do we already have an expiration date?

CHAPTER THIRTY

HARRISON

THE DINNER PARTY'S A SUCCESS. Emery spends the entire evening laughing and moving from person to person, her smile lighting up the entire room. She reintroduces me to her friends/former roommates, who are much kinder to me now than they were at her apartment. They're also rather funny, and Sherri in particular has lots of questions about the building.

"Did you buy this place finished or was it a gut rehab? Who was your architect? Is this marble imported? Are the hardwoods original? God, what history. Have you done any research into the former occupants? Man, this place is incredible!"

We also talk about how she's getting a degree in architecture, though the process is a bit slower because she works twelve-hour days at a trio of Manhattan restaurants to make ends meet.

"But I'll get that degree somehow," she swears to me, and I admire the spark in her eye. "And then one day, people will be asking me about the buildings I made."

"I don't doubt that," I tell her. "With your nerve, I bet you can accomplish anything."

That makes her grin, and I look over her shoulder to catch Emery watching us from afar. She's got her hands full keeping an eye on Ramon's daughter. I suppose I should have made this a childfree dinner, but apparently, those don't exist once you've settled down.

Dinner itself is delicious. Seared scallops in brown butter and lemon sauce, cauliflower Bolognese, savory brussels sprouts, and steaks brought in fresh from New York's finest butchers. There's more, but I barely have time to register or taste it. I'm too busy watching Emery as she talks to Sandy and Ramon, her hands moving through the air as she gesticulates. She glances at me and smiles, waving me on to continue my chat with her friends.

I do, mostly about what they love about New York, what brought them here. They've each got their own story, but through it all, it's easy to see why Emery gravitated towards them. They're all people of grit and determination, and I admire that in them. And I admire it in Emery, too.

Later, once everyone's finally left and I've generously tipped the staff, Emery and I take a long shower together and then fall into bed. It's nothing but domestic light cuddling tonight, and somehow, it's perfect. Just being with her, close to her, is enough. I fall asleep to the sound of her easy breathing, savoring her happiness.

———

WHEN I WAKE up the next morning, she's still asleep. That girl can sleep like a rock when she's tired. I slip out of bed so that I don't disturb her and pull on my robe, and then I call the doorman and ask him to bring the newspapers to me so I don't need to go out. I decide to start with the *Times*, and settle in at the kitchen table with freshly poured coffee.

About forty minutes later, Emery emerges from the bedroom. She's already showered, her hair still damp. She's pulled on some jean shorts and a T-shirt, and her doe eyes go wide at the coffee.

"Ugh, yes, gimme," she says, grabbing a mug and filling it to the brim. "Thank you, caffeine gods."

I chuckle. "How'd you sleep?"

"Great, apparently," she says, sipping the coffee. "Though I'm not used to sleeping in this late on a Saturday."

"Late?" I ask. "It's nine a.m."

"Yeah, but normally, I'd have to be getting my laundry together by now," she says. "You know, to go to the laundromat."

I blink at her.

She sighs as she looks over at the fresh laundry that's stacked neatly by the door, a fresh sprig of lavender on top.

"But I guess I don't need to do that."

I nod. She doesn't have to do that anymore. Shouldn't she be happy?

"I'm just at loose ends here! Everything's done for me. I'm used to spending half the day at the laundromat on Saturdays, then the other half running errands. This is just weird."

"Good weird?" I ask.

"I don't know," she says. "I guess?"

If I cast my mind back far enough, I can remember the days when someone who wasn't me didn't fetch my laundry or clean my house or stock my fridge. But those days are long gone for me, and I guess I've taken for granted that some things just appear like magic for me and not for others.

"I mean, what do you even *do* with a Saturday when it's completely and totally free?"

Her eyes look at me as she says this, and I hold up the newspaper in my hand.

"I read the paper. Prepare for the next week."

She laughs. "How incredibly boring. All this time to yourself, and you use it to avoid spending time with yourself? Unreal."

I tilt my head and consider this. I'd never thought of it that way. I thought of it as getting a jump on the week and being informed about the world. Isn't that what Emery was saying she used to do? Laundry and budget to get ready for Monday. I'm doing the same thing in my own way.

But one look at her raised eyebrow and I know she won't appreciate that answer. I fold the newspaper.

"Fine," I say. "What would *you* like to do on this Saturday?"

Her eyes go wide, and oh no. This was definitely the wrong question to ask. That fact is confirmed by the inhuman squeal that suddenly fills the room.

"Oh man," she says. "Do I have a list of things for us to do."

There's something about the glint in her eye that tells me I'm not going to like these ideas, but it doesn't matter.

It's her.

And whatever she wants to do, I'm in.

———

IT TURNS out that what Emery wants to do is play New York City tourist. She even pulls out a guidebook for New York she's had stashed in her nightstand and hands it to me. It's got little sticky notes sticking out of the corner of nearly every page, and I'm literally speechless as she explains.

"The pink sticky notes are my must dos," she says. "The blue are my really, really, really hope to dos. The green are if I get to it dos. And the yellow are the ones I've already done."

There are approximately forty pink sticky notes and two yellow ones. I would groan, but with the way Emery's smiling, I know I don't have a choice.

"We'll do it all," I say. "Today."

"Really?" Emery asks. "But you hate New York tourist-y stuff."

"I never said that."

"You didn't have to," she says with a laugh. "I can read it all over your face."

"We just have to do it the right way," I tell her. "Give me a few minutes to shower and then make some calls, and then we'll do it all. I promise."

She kisses me softly, her eyelashes fluttering against my cheek as she pulls me into a hug. Then, in a flurry, she's pulling back and looking down at her outfit.

"I need good shoes," she says. "And SPF."

While she handles that, I take care of the arrangements. I call Leo and ask him to meet us downstairs, and then I get ready.

By the time we're in the car, Emery's jittery with excitement.

"I've been wanting to do this since before I even got here," she says. "But it was all so expensive, and I didn't want to go by myself."

"Well, get ready, because we're starting big," I say, pointing out of the window. "We're starting with her."

She rolls the window down and looks out of it, scanning for what I'm talking about. And then she sees it, or rather, she sees her. The Statue of Liberty. She screams.

"Ms. Mills," Leo asks from the front seat. "Should I be expecting a lot of screeching? If so, I'll put in my earplugs."

She laughs, embarrassed, and Leo smiles. "Only kidding, Ms. Mills. Scream away."

Leo pulls into the lot at Battery Park, and Emery practically bounces out of the car as soon as the car's pulled to a stop. I thank Leo and follow her as she sprints to the ferry entrance, ready to wait in line.

"Mr. Duke, Ms. Mills," a man says, waving us over. "Right this way."

We're ushered to the front of the line, and we climb onto the ferry with several eager couples and families. One of the children seems to see it as his personal mission to scream louder than Emery did in the car, but I do my best to tune him out and focus on her.

She must catch me wincing, though, because she smiles at me.

"Kids are pretty loud, huh?"

I shrug. "Seems so."

I don't tell her that what I'm more concerned about is the kid that's trying to launch himself overboard at the moment, or the kid running up and down the deck. That's a falling hazard just waiting to happen.

She bites her lip like she wants to say more, but she doesn't. I take her hand and lead her to the edge of the ferry, where we watch the Statue of Liberty grow tall and infinite in our approach.

"I'd face a thousand screaming kids to be here with you," I tell her. "Especially to see you look like this."

She blushes, and I kiss her. She smiles against my lips, and then we both turn back to face the island.

From there, the day's a blur of different moments. Grabbing hot dogs from a cart, which might honestly end up being Emery's favorite part. I joke with her that she's a cheap date as she gobbles down two of them layered with ketchup, mustard, and pickles. From there, we visit Times Square and Rockefeller Center. Near the end of the afternoon, Emery raids a cart of souvenirs, grabbing the most ridiculous items she can find. One of them is a tight cotton tee that says "I <3 New York" in big red letters, and she pulls it over the shirt she was wearing and grins at me.

"Look! I'm a real New Yorker now."

I can't help but laugh. We stop back at my place so we can change for the evening. I've had new dresses bought for her to choose from, and she squeals over all of them. For dinner, I take her to St. Cloud atop The Knickerbocker Hotel. From our private table, she can see all of New York. The server tells us about how the martini was apparently invented at this very restaurant in 1906, something Emery loves. We sip martinis and she gushes about the day.

"It's not over yet," I tell her. "And unfortunately, we only hit about a third of your sticky notes."

"That's okay," she tells me. "We've got time to do all of it."

She winks. I should hate this, all this tourist-y bullshit, but I don't. Because she takes everything and somehow, changes it.

Our last stop is Broadway, where we take our private box seats for *Hamilton*. Emery's in awe the entire time, gripping my hand. When a tear rolls down her cheek at the end, I wipe it away with my finger.

"This was perfect, you know that, right?" Emery whispers to me as the curtain falls.

"Better than laundry?"

She laughs. "Infinitely better than laundry."

CHAPTER THIRTY-ONE

EMERY

OKAY, so there are some perks to having a billionaire boyfriend. Beyond him being the nicest, sweetest, sexiest man alive, he also gave me a tour of New York that I'll never forget.

I'm still riding a high when I head back to the gym on Sunday for another hip-hop class. I don't even mind Bruce accompanying me. I hate to admit it, but this driver thing is a pretty sweet gig. I can stare out the windows and people watch for as long as I want, and Bruce and I can have arguments about college football.

I'm not that into college football, but I know a little bit about it because my mom's a die-hard Kansas State Wildcats fan. Bruce, for whatever reason, is a Clemson fan. We argue about offense and defense and trades—mostly so I can annoy him—and I discover that he's a pretty funny guy. I still wish he didn't have to wait outside my gym class like a bodyguard, but I know it's coming from a good place.

And damn if it's not convenient.

Doesn't mean I can't be a teensy bit annoyed, though.

Luckily, I've got class to help me get out some of my feelings. Diana's the instructor again, and she puts us through the most intense warm-up of my life. There are a *lot* of what she calls "hip-hop burpees," which means they're basically just burpees that you have to do really, really fast and on beat.

"Keep up, Em," she calls at me when she sees me slacking on a jump. "Put those fingers all the way up in the air when you jump up."

Devil woman. I wanted cardio this morning, not to choke on my own lungs.

Then she pushes us through high knees and a series of jabs. I came for fun dance moves to Salt-N-Pepa, not torture.

We do eventually move into some dance combinations, and those, as usual, are what I love. We do a bunch of spins and drops, pump our hips from side to side, and I even manage to master a footwork sequence that is normally way beyond my level. Diana gifts me with a rare nod of approval, which is huge. William also gives me a nod once or twice, but those aren't rare. If anything, he gives one too many.

I'm not surprised William's in class or that he's paying extra attention to me. He's been pretty friendly with me when I've come after work this past week, but I haven't really had much time for talking since they were weeknights. As we're wrapping up the last combination, though, I can tell that he's making a beeline for me.

"Emery," he says with a big grin. He's wearing one of those tank tops with giant holes cut for the sleeves, so I get a clear view of his six-pack from the side. Honestly, though, my eyes don't even linger. Harrison is a thousand times sexier.

"Hey William," I say, mopping up my sweat with a towel. Diana didn't cut us a single break today, and my body's screaming at me to sit down. Or collapse. Same difference at this point.

"Want to get a smoothie? My treat."

I mostly want to get back home, especially since I've got a big week ahead of me at work and Sundays are for relaxing. You know, after the hip-hop torture.

Still, there's nothing wrong with getting a smoothie with the guy. He knows I have a boyfriend, and he's respected that boundary, just like he promised he would.

"Sure," I say. "Let's go."

We head to the smoothie bar, and I order a strawberry-banana-kale thing while William orders something that sounds like it's about ninety percent protein powder, ten percent grass. Ugh. I'm all for healthy eating, but I draw the line at anything that looks like it came out of a lawnmower.

"So," he says. "You started your new job this week, right? How's it going?"

I grin. "It's amazing. I'm really loving it. My coworkers are awesome, and we're starting this incredible project. I can't believe I get to be a part of it."

He nods. "That sounds cool. Say, I don't think you ever told me... Where are you working, exactly?"

I swallow a gulp of my smoothie. Asking where I work isn't overly personal. It's hardly a secret. All my former roomies know where I work. It's normal to talk about your job.

But there's something about the way William just asked that makes it feel just a little sketchy. But I'm probably just getting paranoid. All of Harrison's talk about New York being dangerous, probably.

"Duke Capital," I say finally. "Do you know of it?"

William's eyes widen, and he shakes his head.

"What?" I ask, confused. He looks like I just told him that I kick puppies in my spare time.

"That's Harrison Duke's company, isn't it?"

I nod, a little confused about why that matters. I'm surely not about to tell him that Harrison's my boyfriend. Not when he's reacting and looking like that.

"I just...I'm not a big fan of the guy, that's all."

I bite my lip. I'm fighting the urge to defend Harrison and also keep my mouth shut because I want to know why he feels that way. I try to think of what Harrison would do. He'd probably play things close to the vest and let William reveal what he knows, and then he'd go from there. That's the boss move here.

I lean back, sipping my smoothie. "Do you, uh, know him? Harrison Duke, I mean."

Another laugh from William, this one low and bitter.

"Yeah," he says. "Unfortunately. Not personally, but professionally."

Who is William? Maybe I should've tried to find out more about him before I agreed to be his gym buddy. Now I'm wondering how I can ask without sounding like I'm awkwardly prying.

"Really?" I say, still playing like I didn't wake up this morning in Harrison's bed. "That sounds intense."

For a second, William doesn't say anything. It's like he's deciding whether or not to tell me something. He leans back and tosses back some of his green sludge.

"I can't believe you work for that guy," he says at last. "If you want to know the truth, he took my family's company from me and destroyed it. He's a dream destroyer. And I'm hardly the only one. Be careful working there. You'll lose your soul too, if you stay there, justifying one thing after another."

Seriously? It's not that I think William's lying. I'm sure he has his own version about whatever happened. But saying my soul's at risk? It sounds like he's laying it on a little thick, and I decide I definitely don't trust him.

Part of me wonders if he actually does know, somehow, that Harrison's my boyfriend. Is this his way of trying to hit on me or draw a wedge between us? Well, that definitely won't work. I'll get my information from the source, thank you very much.

"That sounds awful," I say. "I'll be careful."

William doesn't look convinced.

"Just watch your back," he says. "You're the kind of girl he would chew up and spit back out."

Now I really hate this dude. I'm the kind of girl who can go toe to toe with Harrison, actually. A girl he respects. A girl he cares about. A girl he believes in. A girl he went all the way to Kansas to retrieve.

"Thanks for the advice," I say. "But I've got to be going."

"Wait, Emery—"

But I don't wait. I take my smoothie and go, not looking back.

I've got better things to do with my time than listen to weirdos at the gym and their bullshit.

CHAPTER THIRTY-TWO

HARRISON

MONDAYS ARE MADE MUCH BETTER by the fact that they start with Emery. She insists we eat an actual breakfast, and she loves to ask me questions about the day ahead and pick my brain about meetings she has lined up. She'll ask about someone's personality and strategies to deal with them. It shows that I was right to promote her because she's paying attention to all the right things. And I won't lie. Her asking my opinion, knowing she trusts me and sees me as an expert? It's definitely a fucking turn-on.

Which means that most of my days also start with sex. I walk into work with a goddamn pep in my step, which is ridiculous but worth it.

"Something fun planned today?" Sandy asks me when I walk in, a knowing smile on her face. She thinks I'm looking forward to something, when really, I'm remembering Emery's face as I fucked her in the shower this morning. The way her head rolled back as she gasped my name.

"Do meetings count as fun?" I deflect, and Sandy laughs in response.

"Well, your first one's with Ramon, so it can't be that bad," Sandy says. "Here's your coffee."

She hands me a mug, and I head into my office where Ramon's already waiting. He looks tired but happy, which I'm starting to think is how he's going to look until those kids of his turn eighteen. He sits up as I put my briefcase down on my desk.

"Well, boss, I did what you asked. I've got a great lead for you."

I take a sip of my coffee. "Yeah? Anything more promising than the duds everyone brought in last week?"

"Actually, I think so," he says. "It's a small start-up for now, but I think they've got major potential. They're based here in New York. It's all about local artists and giving back to the community, and I think that's right up our alley."

I nod, considering it. "Tell me more."

"Well, I know we're keeping a close eye on our image in regards to which charities we support," Ramon says. "You know. In case…well, in case certain things transpire."

He's talking around the subject, but we both know he's talking about Blythe. Claire might've been able to end the marriage, but I'm the one that's still got to figure out a way to remove her from the company in a way that minimizes the damage. And judging by the smirks she's given me the two times I've seen her in the lobby, she knows I'm in between a rock and a hard place.

I won't say it to Ramon, at least not yet, but it worries me. I don't want her to be able to do any more harm than she already has.

But apparently, I don't need to say it to Ramon, because he's already a few steps ahead of me.

"I had someone look into Blythe's deals on the down low," he says. "And also Robert. And, I'll be honest Harrison. I'm concerned."

I sigh, rubbing my temples as I stand and look down at New York from my window.

"Don't sugarcoat it, Ramon," I say. "Just tell me what you found out."

"Well, the good news is that I think we'll be able to relieve Blythe of her charity duties," he says. "I think I've found enough to leverage an agreement in which she'll step down. As far as her shares in the company go, though, I don't think we'll be able to get those. And Robert's got his hands all over them."

"Which means he profits off of you," he adds, unnecessarily.

Months ago, this would've been a stab to my heart that Blythe would have delighted in. A way for her to take shares of my own company away from me. But now, it's just money. What I want is to keep my business on the right track, and part of that is fixing the damage Blythe has done with the charity division. I want it fixed, not because of the image issues, but because it's the right thing to do.

"That's fine." I nod, waving my hand for him to continue. "But something tells me that that's not the bad news you've been hiding."

I look back at Ramon. He sits forward in the chair he's sitting in and rubs the stubble on his face. Looking at him closer, I see that he looks more tired than usual.

"Ramon, is everything okay? Not with the company. But with you?"

He smiles. "Yeah, it is, actually. Really great. Anita's pregnant again."

My eyes bulge. Three? Wow. "Congratulations, man."

"Thanks," he says. "She was up late last night with some morning sickness, but it'll pass soon. Which reminds me... Sorry that Cesar was a little terror the other night at your dinner party. When he gets going, he's just nonstop."

I wave it off. "Don't worry about that. All my shit is replaceable, your kids aren't. He was just making me anxious reminding me of every sharp corner and piece of glass in my apartment. I was imagining eighteen different ways he could maim himself while in my apartment, but I'm sure you're worried about that shit all the time. Kids are fucking terrifying."

I remember worrying about the kids on the ferry falling overboard again and shudder. Why would a person so casually put all of their heart into something so fragile and then act so cavalier about it?

Then, I wince, realizing how that must've sounded to a man who's just told me that his wife's pregnant with another kid.

"Sorry," I say quickly. "I didn't mean—"

"Don't apologize," he says. "It is fucking terrifying. All of it. But it's also the best thing I've ever done with my life."

"Better than working with me at Duke?" I say sarcastically. "I'm hurt."

He laughs. "Yes, and I'll stand by that, even to my boss. Hell, parenting makes *me* a better person. It'll make you better too, if you and Emery decide to go that route..."

I look back out at New York bustling beneath me. "We'll see."

"Anyway," Ramon says. "The bad news is that someone's still up to something. You must've pissed them off when you managed to hold on to Pink. I'm hearing rumors about a pending attack on our image. They've got some hit jobs about you that they might be trying to run in the tabloids."

"Sounds desperate," I say, thinking out loud. "And more like it's been planted to scare me rather than anything else."

"I think it's as good a reason as any to keep finding businesses to invest in that are doing good in the world," he says.

"Ramon, we're doing that because it's the right thing to do."

He laughs. "I agree with you, but when did Harrison Duke become so noble?"

I think about Emery. It's been that way ever since her.

"I've always been semi-noble," I say instead. "But yeah, let's look into this business. I like it."

Ramon nods and stands up. "Will do."

"And Ramon?"

"Yes, sir?"

"Why don't you leave a little early today? I'm sure your wife could use the help."

Ramon laughs. "Harrison, she's only in her first trimester, so she's still at work, but I appreciate the offer."

He's still laughing when he leaves my office. Still, I'm glad to have Ramon on my side. We might be living in completely different worlds, but I know he's coming from the right place for my company. For too long I was focused on building something that I forgot why I was building it in the first place. It wasn't just because I wanted my own empire or to make something of my own. Or maybe that's what it was initially, but now, I see it clearly.

Duke Capital's going to make a difference in the world, and like everything else in my life, I'm going to see to it. Personally.

CHAPTER THIRTY-THREE

EMERY

YOU KNOW ALL that advice about how to start the day off on the right foot? Mom told me that the key to a good day was to always, no matter what, make your bed. Like, she said that as long as I made my bed, everything in the world would turn out all right. Making a bed, at least to my mom, was the prevention to having a bad day.

Blogs and news article like to say it starts with breakfast, which I do agree with. I don't know when Harrison decided that he could start the day with a protein bar and a cup of coffee, but he's wrong. That's not breakfast. That's barely food. And Harrison has literally no excuse. He has a personal chef, so I've been insisting that we have breakfast. We've been experimenting for days to see if any one breakfast over another impacts our day. Omelets, scrambled eggs, eggs benedict, avocado toast, waffles, oatmeal. You name it and we're trying it.

However, I think that everyone, including my mom, have totally held back on the real secret to starting the morning right.

It's sex.

Hands down, no debate.

Specifically, sex with Harrison.

On this day, I wake to a trail of kisses being pressed against my skin from my shoulder to my hand. The movements are so soft, that at first, I think I'm dreaming. Then, I feel him curved against me, spooning me from behind, and I realize that I'm definitely not dreaming. The hardness of his erection presses against my back, and I wake up with a small moan.

"Good morning," he says as I turn around.

"Someone's ready to start the day with a bang," I murmur, snuggling closer.

"See, I knew you were right for marketing. Not even awake for five minutes and you're already whipping out the puns."

I laugh, and he captures my mouth in a kiss. This isn't a soft kiss. It's one that's hungry, and as soon as my hand finds his cock, I can tell why. He's hard and throbbing in my hand, and he groans into our kiss.

"I dreamed about you all night," he says, nipping at my ear. "And then when I woke up, you were just sleeping away."

I laugh, but it turns into a moan as he kisses my neck.

"Well this is always an excellent way to wake me up," I tell him, and I fist his hard cock in my hand, moving up and down as he leans into my touch.

His hand finds my breast and cups it through my nightshirt. My nipples harden at his touch, and he rolls the sensitive tip in his fingers through the fabric, making me sigh with pleasure.

He kisses me again, this time on my mouth. I part my lips, letting his tongue slip into my mouth so that I can taste him. He must've already gotten up to have his coffee, and I grin thinking of how he came back to bed because he wanted me. I love how he wants me.

He pulls back and looks at me with lust-filled eyes. "How are you this perfect in the morning?"

I answer with a tug on his cock, and he groans at the movement. Heat pools between my legs in response, wanting him inside of me, but I force myself to wait. I like to see how far I can push Harrison to the edge before I let him have me. How wild I can make him.

I throw the sheets off of me and crawl on top of him, dipping my chest and shoulders forward so that my ass is curved and visible in the air as I move to kiss his chest and drag my tongue down the hard plane of his abs. His cock twitches upward, hitting me in the stomach, and I move down until the tender, hard flesh is between my tits. He fists his hands in the sheets as I move my upper body forward and back, dragging my nipples across his stomach while his cock slides between my breasts.

"You fucking devil," he says, and I smile my most innocent smile before sliding down further and capturing the tip of his cock in my mouth.

I love a lot of things about Harrison, but I'll admit that his cock is near the top. I love how he feels in my mouth, the way my tongue can make him shiver with pleasure. I take him as far into my throat as I can, letting the tip bump against the back of my tongue, and then I pull away, dragging my tongue along the underside of his dick as I go. Then I swirl around the tip, swallowing the pre-cum there, making his hips jerk upward.

This is the part I love. How far will he hold off until he just can't resist me another moment. It's my favorite game, and now, I get to play it every morning.

He doesn't last long before he lifts my chin up, the tip of his cock still in my mouth as I meet his eyes with mine. I pop his dick out of my mouth and grin.

With a single move, he rolls me over so that he's on top,

and I gasp at the sudden power change. I reach out to grab him again, but he shakes his head.

"Your turn," he says.

And then his mouth drops to my stomach, kissing my hipbones and down my thighs until he reaches his ultimate destination. He swirls his tongue in circles near my entrance, teasing me with that fantastic tongue of his. Then, he's plunging inside of me, in and out as he works me with his tongue until I'm nearly incoherent. Meanwhile, one of his hands travels up my stomach and circles my nipple, and then his tongue finds my clit. The motions combined undo me, and my orgasm shakes through me, a bolt of sudden, electric pleasure.

I'm still short of breath when he sits up and wipes his mouth, his cock hard as he hovers over me.

"I want you," I tell him. "Please. Now."

I grab his face and lower him to me, kissing him hungrily, loving the feel of his slick cock pressed between us. I use my hand to guide him to my still swollen clit, tapping the head of his cock against me, so close to being inside me that it seems unjustifiably unfair.

"Easy now," he says with a little laugh. "I've got to get the condom."

"Condoms are really slowing our roll."

He smirks at me as he leans over to the nightstand. "Not as much as the alternative would."

Right.

He slides on the condom, and then he's kissing me again, but it isn't enough. I need him inside of me. I grab his cock and tug him towards me, and he gets the hint and lowers himself into position. Then, his lips still on mine, he slides inside of me, and every fiber of my being feels electrified in the best possible way.

Yes. This is exactly, without a doubt, the best way to start the day. Because even after we finish, the warm afterglow follows me. It follows me to the shower, to breakfast, out the door, and even into the office. No one knows exactly why I'm smiling, and it doesn't matter. What matters is that I carry it with me the entire day.

I know it's not just the sex. It's the intimacy and the trust and the confidence. The joy.

But there's no denying that the sex is great, too.

Still, though, I have an idea for how to make it even better.

I put a client lunch on my calendar today. Which is a tiny little white lie. I wouldn't have to make little white lies if it weren't for Bruce. After work, he's with me wherever I go, so if I'm going to make a run for it, lunch is my best option. Because damn, even though I love having a driver, when a girl needs to do something a little undercover, it's more of a hassle than climbing out my bedroom window back in Kansas was.

Part of me resents that I have to do this, pretending to have a client meeting that I don't have. It reminds me that, as much as I think I have freedom, it's not as boundless as I'd like it to be. The words from Blythe re-enter my mind, followed closely by that creeper, William, from the gym. I haven't seen him since our last interaction, but I also forgot to mention him to Harrison.

Not that it matters. I know he was lying. And I also know that Harrison's coming from the right place when he tries to protect me. We're going to have to figure out a balance, and I'm confident that we will. After all, what broke Blythe and Harrison apart wasn't that he was controlling. It was because Blythe took his trust and completely detonated it. That will never be our problem.

Still, he does need to understand a few things. I have wings, and I'm determined to spread them. My afternoon today is, in a way, a start. A step toward having more say. More control over myself.

I grab a cab since the place I'm going isn't too far away.

It's not nearly as nice as the car Bruce carts me around town in, but there's something exciting about an illicit cab ride. My driver's an older man who asks me how long I've lived here, and when I tell him not long, he's thrilled to talk about how I settled in. Born and bred in New York himself, he tells me.

"I'm still getting used to everything," I tell him honestly. "But I love it."

He grins at me in the rearview mirror. "Definitely beats the small town, doesn't it?"

Yes, random cab driver. It most definitely does.

———

THE CAB DROPS me off outside a huge building, one that's a dime a dozen in New York. Black steel that stretches upward higher than seems mathematically possible. I take a deep breath at the sight of it.

Here's the next step of Emery Mills seizing control and taking her life by the reins.

Because while my new life 2.0 started with me landing a real job at Duke Capital, my future's only just begun. If I'm going to live my life the way I want to, I need to be the kind of girl who sees a problem and figures out the solution. And right now, I've got a problem. One I should've solved a while ago. Like, as soon as I landed back in New York.

I head inside the building and take the elevator up to the tenth floor. Locating the office I'm in search of, I enter, finding modern décor and soft landscape paintings. I walk up to the reception desk and write my name on the clipboard.

She smiles at me. "And who are you seeing today, Miss?"

"Dr. Gonzalez," I say. "For Emery Mills."

"We'll get you checked in right away," she says.

Back in Kansas, I had to drive to the slightly larger neighboring town to see my doctor. It was a total hassle, and it was a little awkward because everyone knew everybody, including your doctor. Even though I knew she wasn't legally allowed to say anything to anyone about me, I still felt kind of weird. I'm already loving the difference in New York, and I'm awarding extra points for the convenience and the fact that the doctor who is examining me today is not going to see my mom later at a bake-off.

I'm called back pretty quickly, which is great since I'm trying to sneak this appointment into a lunch hour. They give me a cup to pee in, which I do quickly thanks to all the coffee I drank this morning, and then I'm taken back to Dr. Gonzalez's office. I'm given the cloth gown with the open butt design and the "privacy paper." What, exactly, is the point of the privacy paper in this situation? I'm going to have my feet in stirrups showing everything I've got to this woman in less than ten minutes. But whatever. I fold the paper over myself and wait in the drafty room for the doctor.

When I was looking for a gynecologist, I was sort of shocked at the sheer number of them that I could choose from. Another benefit to a city this big: lots of choices. I narrowed it down to doctors accepting both new patients and my new health care plan thanks to my permanent employment and found Dr. Gonzalez. She had a friendly face and said on her website that she was there to make the patient's life easier. Which is excellent and how all doctors should operate, in my opinion.

Dr. Gonzalez comes in and is just as friendly as her picture suggests. Her black hair's tied back in a ponytail, and she shakes my hand and gives me a friendly smile.

"So, Ms. Mills," she says. "What're you in for today?"

"I'd like to go on birth control," I tell with probably more excitement than is necessary. It's just, this is new for me and I am fairly excited about it. I've been thinking about this for over a week. Another step in me taking control of my future. And it's going to be a great surprise for Harrison. No more annoying condoms. Ugh, I cannot even think about how he'll react to this news because I'll start blushing on the exam table.

His reaction is gonna be amazing though.

Guaranteed.

And this appointment is running so on schedule I think I can squeeze in a trip to some kind of sex store before I head back to the office. I'll get some cute undies, or something like edible lube. Actually, I don't have a clue what I should buy, but I'll google a nearby store when I get out of here and go wild when I get there. I need to take advantage of not having Bruce with me while I can, after all.

This is going to be the best surprise ever.

"Ms. Mills? Did you hear me?"

I realize that I got so excited thinking about the sex store that I sort of tuned out the doctor. Which, oops. I should probably pay attention. Definitely should.

"Sorry," I say. "I'm a little excited. I think I want the pill, though I'm open to other options, too. I'm in a committed relationship and we're just past condoms, you know? Since we're exclusive and all that. And they're so inconvenient." I finish this little speech in a rush. Probably more than she needs to know.

Dr. Gonzalez's eyes widen a bit before she pulls a stool closer and sits, her face is the picture of doctorly impartiality but also…concerned?

"Okay," she says, crossing her legs and settling a file chart on her lap. "Well, that's good."

"Right. It's good! And he's the absolute nicest—wait," I cut myself off. I can't ignore the weird vibe I'm getting from Dr. Gonzalez any longer. "It's good," I repeat for lack of anything else to say.

"Well, we ran the urine sample, and it sounds like you might be in for a bit of a surprise," she says gently as if giving me a moment to prepare myself.

I blink at her. Do I have a UTI or something? Because that

would really suck. We'd probably have to skip sex for like, an entire week.

Dr. Gonzalez takes a breath, and then she smiles.

"Ms. Mills," she says. "You're pregnant."

The Billionaire's Intern Trilogy concludes with The Billionaire's Promise.

The Billionaire's Promise is a classic former-virgin-marries-billionaire romance - if your idea of classic is extra-spicy angst, straight-up with a twist that will leave you more than satisfied...

No one saw this coming.

Least of all me.

When she dumped coffee on me in my own lobby, I sure had no plans to put a ring on my intern's finger. I didn't even expect to learn her name.

Apparently I didn't get my own memo.

She screwed me, screwed me over, and somehow managed to steal my heart in the process.

Emery is a shark in kitten's clothing. The only woman I can guarantee will never bore me. She couldn't care less about my brownstone. My money. My last name. Which is exactly why I'm ready to share them all with her.

Well, that and the mindblowing bedroom activities.

Although we've never needed a bed.

Do you take this woman?

Oh, I'm ready to *take* her... over and over and over again.

I've been married before. But doing it with this little hellcat? I'd give everything up to build a future with her. To have a family.

But I'm not the only one with a claim to Emery's future...

Get The Billionaire's Promise.

PAIGE PRESS

Paige Press isn't just Laurelin Paige anymore…

Laurelin Paige has expanded her publishing company to bring readers even more hot romances.

Sign up for our newsletter to get the latest news about our releases and receive a free book from one of our amazing authors:

Stella Gray
CD Reiss
Jenna Scott
Raven Jayne
JD Hawkins
Poppy Dunne

ALSO BY LIA HUNT

The Billionaire's Intern Trilogy

The Billionaire's Intern

The Billionaire's Mistake

The Billionaire's Promise

ABOUT THE AUTHOR

Lia Hunt is a pen name for two writers who adore billionaires and virgins with scorching love scenes, jaw-dropping cliffhangers, and swoony happy endings.

Made in United States
North Haven, CT
15 June 2022

20281319R00129